D0865576

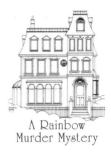

A Rainbow
Murder Mystery

Mystery at Clareton Manor

by

KATHLEEN NEWBERG

Rainbow Books, Inc.
FLORIDA

Library of Congress Cataloging-in-Publication Data

Newberg, Kathleen, 1947-
   Mystery at Clareton Manor / by Kathleen Newberg.— 1st ed.
      p. cm.
   ISBN-13: 978-1-56825-105-9 (trade pbk. : alk. paper)
   ISBN-10: 1-56825-105-X (trade pbk. : alk. paper)
   I. Title.
   PS3614.E566M97 2006
   813'.6—dc22

                                                2005019367

Mystery at Clareton Manor
Copyright © 2006 Kathleen Newberg
ISBN-13: 978-1-56825-105-9
ISBN-10: 1-56825-105-X

Published by
Rainbow Books, Inc.
P. O. Box 430
Highland City, FL 33846-0430
www.RainbowBooksInc.com

Editorial Offices and Wholesale/Distributor Orders
Telephone (863) 648-4420
Email: RBIbooks@aol.com
www.RainbowBooksInc.com

Individuals' Orders
Toll-free Telephone (800) 431-1579
www.BookCH.com

First edition 2006

12 11 10 09 08 07 06   5 4 3 2 1

Printed in the United States of America.

To my mother,
Alma Frances Graham Newberg.
She loved life.

Contents

PART I: ARRIVAL

PART II: WHERE'S HARVEY?

PART III: MOLLY'S MUDDLE

Cast of Characters

Molly May, a retired chief detective and a highly sensitive person

Harvey and Abigail Ruger, a wealthy couple from Spartanburg. An industrial baron, Mr. Ruger had accumulated many enemies along with a vast fortune over thirty years in business

Erika Bischoff, a German immigrant, who had worked hard for many years to save enough money to open a small country spa

Christa and Peter Bischoff, Erika's two adult children, who lived in the village and helped out at the spa

Marian and Francis Whitt, from Charleston. Marian was Abigail Ruger's sister but rarely saw her because of tension between their spouses

Nora Pritchard, vice president of New East Airlines, tall, slim, pinched-looking, with hair cropped too short, and a sensational wardrobe

Barry Kholer, a former stockbroker, now a part-time massage therapist at the spa

Tony Ruger, Harvey and Abigail's irresponsible, playboy son

Cindy Celina, Tony's *l'amour de jour*

Ernie Snail, the weasel-faced, nasal-toned gardener who spent more time looking for ways to avoid work than he did working

Marcus and Angie Bella, a young black couple, enthusiastically spending a stock market windfall

Randy Yazid, the Indian cook

Chantal, the cook's helper

Dale Stromb, the pastor of a small Clareton church with declining membership, a neighbor of the spa

Detective Bloom, the village law officer who tried to solve the mystery

Officer Windham, a village policeman

Part I

Arrival

A kindhearted woman gains respect,
but ruthless men gain only wealth.

Proverbs 11:16

1
Making Ready

It was an ordinary sunny Saturday afternoon in mid-April. Spring flowers in a variety of vivid colors were in full bloom, and the trees and grass were the lovely lime green of early spring. Ernie Snale, the head grounds-keeper, wandered idly from the potter's shed to a small stand of peach trees that needed tending. Ernie was known to be a bit lazy, to say the least, and at the busiest times of the year, additional gardening services had to be hired from the nearby village of Clareton. He managed the barest necessary maintenance for the yard and garden.

Pausing to squint at the sun to gauge its position in its arc above him, he then glanced around the earth to evaluate the size and shape of the shadows; he judged it must be at least three o'clock. The sidewalk in front of the house was still to be edged, and there were branches to be picked up off the back lawn and discarded; he was eager to finish up and leave by five. Normally he did not work on Saturday, but guests would be arriving early on Monday morning for the start of a one-week spa retreat. Mrs. Bischoff, his employer and the spa owner, had asked him to come in just long enough to tidy up the yard and surrounding areas. So far he'd managed to fritter away

3

half the day. ". . . better get busy if I don't want to miss happy hour," he muttered to himself.

Ernie worked at the Clareton Manor Wellness Spa, owned and managed by Mrs. Erika Bischoff. Built well over one hundred years ago on land enhanced by natural hot springs, the modified estate house now housed a spa that offered a wide variety of personal services to promote relaxation, stress reduction, weight control, health, and general fitness, or so said the colorful brochure adorned with beautiful smiling young men and women. The lush landscape boasted in the photographs in the brochure was under Ernie's care, but it was only with additional professional lawn care services that it kept its inviting appearance. This time of year hundreds of azaleas in every color were blooming under the snowy dogwood boughs. It was an appealing scene.

As Ernie resumed his shuffle down the path, a voice called out, "Hey! Ernie!"

Ernie turned and saw Chantal, the young cook's helper. Chantal's services were acquired specifically during spa weeks when lavish, nutritious meals were prepared for ten to twelve guests three times each day. Just nineteen years old with the energy and enthusiasm to match her years, she had a very dark skin, beautiful dark pools for eyes and a shyness about her smile in spite of her exuberance. She was fairly bouncing along beside a bicycle she pushed in Ernie's direction.

"Hey, Chantal," Ernie responded without enthusiasm. "What's up?"

"Oh, nothin'—really. I just saw you headin' out, and I thought I'd walk along. What are you doing here on Saturday?"

"Well, you know, the spa folks'll be comin' on Monday, and Mrs. Bischoff wanted the dead branches pruned out the peach trees and stuff," replied Ernie in his whiney, nasal voice. "The ole bird will be a keepin' us all pretty busy for a while, I 'spect." His sedentary lifestyle supported by an old, worn recliner had helped to produce an unnatural curve in his spine that had resulted in an irregular gait; meanwhile, his arms seemed to dangle from his shoulders as if attached only by threads. His hips were broad, like a matronly woman, caused by years of sitting, which he managed to find time to do even when on the job. His appearance was more grotesque than sinister. "So whatcha up to this afternoon?" he went on.

Chantal seemed inclined to engage him in conversation; she was naturally outgoing and was not above a little gossip now and then. "I'm off to the market. *Mr.* Yazid wants fresh greens for the first big dinner for the guests on Monday night. I'm to find the freshest and best at the farmer's market, whether kale, collards, or turnip greens." Her reference to the head chef as "Mr. Yazid" carried a note of sarcasm. "He's a fine cook, for sure, but there's something about him that's just not right, it seems to me," she added.

"Whatcha mean? I ain't noticed anythin' peculiar about him; he seems like a pretty okay feller to me," came the reply. Ernie squinted at the sun again, reminding himself of the time. The warm, sunny spring day enhanced his natural laziness, and he would rather engage in idle chat than exert himself with gardening chores. Scandal of any sort, about anyone, was his favorite topic, and his ears perked up at the possibility of some juicy tidbit about the reclusive cook.

"Well, he's always snooping around, for one thing. I've even seen him reading Mrs. Bischoff's mail that's been left in the kitchen! What do you think he's looking for?" Randy Yazid, the full-time chef at the Clareton Manor, lived in the little cook's cottage on the spa premises, down a winding trail nearly a quarter mile behind the main house. He was Indian (Middle East, not American) and specialized in his native cuisine, but he had also studied briefly at the Cordon Bleu. Even though he'd been employed at the spa for a little more than two years, none of the other staff seemed to know anything much about him. He rarely associated with the others and never spoke of his family or his past.

"Oh, don' mind him. He's jus' thata way. Don' nobody know nothin' about him, though, fer sure—his family or where he's from. Betcha Randy's not his born name. Randy's more of a Texas cowboy name than an Indian name." Ernie chortled at his unintended pun. "Anyhow, I don' reckon Mrs. Bischoff's got no secrets that he's likely to find in her mail."

Chantal was not reassured. "I don't like the way he looks at me. Sometimes when I turn around in the kitchen, there he is standing there, looking at me. It's spooky." Having lived all her short life in a small South Carolina town, she had never met an Indian before; but there was more to it than that. There was something not just right about Randy Yazid. His avoidance of eye contact had not gone unnoticed by her, and this was something else her youthful naiveté could not explain away.

"I don't know about him, Ernie. He scares me. If you opened him up, I bet there'd be nothin' but maggots inside!" Then with an abrupt change of tone, she added brightly, "I'd better be going, or the farmer's market will be closed before I get there—that'll put me in real trouble." With that, she hopped upon the bicycle she had been pushing and rode away.

"See ya later, Chantal," Ernie called out as he continued down the worn path toward the peach grove, whining under his breath about his burdensome duties. His arms and hands fluttered about him as if on puppet strings.

2

Molly Begins an Adventure

About that same time, some distance away in Columbia, Molly May felt the comforting warmth of the sunlight through the west window on the back of the house as she folded carefully selected items of clothing and packed them into a single suitcase. She was preparing for her first trip since her retirement nearly six months before; Molly was looking forward to it almost with longing. During her working years, she had rarely taken a vacation, not a real one anyway, and the chance to rest and relax at a real spa for a whole week was a welcome and overdue indulgence. It was something she had always dreamed of but never even considered to be a possibility considering her limited means.

The springtime cheered her. It had been a long, cold winter: record-breaking for South Carolina. There had been three significant snows, one with ice that caused widespread power outages; she had been without electrical power for an entire week causing her beloved cottage to seem confining and comfortless. Winter had a way of seeming endless, but when spring broke through, it was if doors of a dungeon had been sprung open. Big puffs of fresh air and buckets of sunshine were dashed about everywhere. And to make it all perfect, she was actually about to indulge herself in the province of the wealthy—a whole week at a real spa.

Molly had been raised on a farm in the country and barely finished high school and that two years late. Not because she was not smart and able to learn quickly—she was—but because she missed weeks of school at a time to help get the seed in the ground in early spring or to get the crop harvested in the fall. She had two brothers, but her father needed all the hands he could get so her gender did not save her from hard farm labor. Her mother had died in childbirth when Molly was only thirteen; the child died also. Always her father's favorite, after her mother's death, Papa, as she called him, was all the more considerate of her; but that did not mean lessening of farm chores on top of cooking and tending house. Hard work was all she had ever known.

Growing up in a household without a mother or any other feminine influence, Molly never learned much about womanly charm and beauty. She had tried to use makeup from time to time but finally gave it up because she could never seem to get it right. She had a pleasant, oval face, but her nose was a little too long and the tip curved under; there was a gap between her two front teeth; she had never been able to afford cosmetic dentistry, not that she would have anyway. Papa always insisted that beauty was only skin deep, and somehow she had come to believe it. Her hair was naturally wavy; she had had it straightened once when straight hair was faddish, but it looked foolish.

Except for church every Sunday, as a young woman she didn't go out much. By the time she was thirty-three, still living with her father on the farm, it was assumed by most everyone, including herself, that she would be an old maid, but then Mr. Bristow, whose wife had died leaving him with a teenaged daughter, came along and wanted to marry her. He was a farm hand who had worked for her father from time to time, and he saw a chance to become a landowner after the two brothers moved away, one to New York and the other to Denver. They were married, and when the old man died, the inheritance came through as expected.

They worked the farm together, but Molly wasn't happy. "Just do as you're told," Mr. Bristow used to say. And she did what she was told, grudgingly, because she saw no way out. These were not days that she looked back upon fondly.

Within a couple of years after acquiring the farm, Mr. Bristow suffered a stroke that paralyzed his entire left side and left him wheelchair bound. His daughter, by then eighteen, moved to town and took a job in a mill. Left to care for her invalid husband and run the farm on her own, Molly was so overwhelmed the first time she drove the tractor out in the middle of a big 12-acre field that she wept, but as time went on, she persevered and learned to repair the tractor as well as to drive it. Her crops were always as good as her neighbors, whose offers of help she politely turned down; she never wanted to depend on anyone else. Year around, her tanned, leathery skin draped over her long, lean limbs. It was a tough life, and it toughened her as well.

After Mr. Bristow died without a will, Molly lost the fifty-acre farm in probate, reverted to her maiden name, and moved to Columbia. Because of her strong, determined physique, she was able to get a job right away as a prison guard at minimum wage. Her hard work and integrity attracted notice, but it was after more than twice the time it took a man to get promoted that she finally began to move up in the ranks. Eventually she moved to the City Police Department, Office of Investigations, where she built a reputation for being one of the best criminal investigators in the State. She thrived in the atmosphere of independence, where no one told her what to do. She ruled herself.

As much as she had enjoyed her work and found it satisfying, it was in the past. Retirement was good; she had heard others say they missed going to work every day after retirement, but she had never felt that way. She stayed busy with gardening, charities, and other hobbies. Her little cottage with spring breezes blowing the curtains at the open windows and her little garden bursting with color demonstrated how good life could be. Her income was quite small, but she had always been thrifty and could manage. Affording a spa vacation was not something she ever envisioned, but her old friend Erika Bischoff had opened a small country spa on a hundred or so acres in Clareton and had invited her for a free visit.

Some twenty years ago Erika had started a career as a massage therapist at a chiropractor's practice, and Molly was one of her first clients. She often spoke of a dream of opening a full-service wellness spa some day, so she worked long hours, lived frugally and saved her pennies to achieve her goal. Finally, with her two children (her husband had abandoned them years ago), she was able to secure enough credit to buy an ancient Manor House in the country. With their own labor and limited subcontracting of specialized tasks, they refurbished it. To buy building materials for the renovation, she sold timber from the acres of woods surrounding the house. Then she and her two children painstakingly planted evergreen trees in perfectly spaced rows and columns that formed neat alleyways that crisscrossed through the woods.

Over the years, Erika had added a two-story wing to the rear of the house and it could now accommodate up to twelve guests at a time in addition to the live-in staff.

Molly thought of Erika's son and daughter whom she had known since they were toddlers. Christa and Peter were adults now; both lived in the nearby village of Clareton and helped out at the spa when their mother had guests. Christa was a certified massage therapist, and Peter was a fitness trainer. With his six-foot-plus frame and bodybuilder physique, Peter could project an ominous presence except for his fair hair and twinkling blue eyes. Christa was tall like her brother and large-boned, lanky, not the "sweet-and-pretty" type that men tend to favor, though she had had a beau or two. Her personality was effervescent: making friends was effortless for her. Both were committed to making their mother's business enterprise a success and were postponing any thought of marriage and their own home ownership until she was well established.

Molly packed lightly for the six-day stay at Erika's Clareton Manor Wellness Spa. She needed only comfortable, casual clothing for everyday wear, a classic navy silk sheath for any formal dinners that might be served, and a surplus of workout clothes. In spite of her age, Molly had maintained the physical fitness she first developed on the farm; she had dabbled in weight training, power yoga, and various other strength training activities. Fitness had been a requirement for her job in law enforcement as well as farming; and even after retirement, she reasoned, one needs sufficient physical strength to perform day-to-day chores, especially when one lives alone and has no one else to perform them.

Placing the last t-shirt into the suitcase, she closed it. Even though the formal spa activities would not begin until Monday, Erika had invited Molly to come a day early so the old friends could catch up on things. She picked up the brochure and looked at it again: hot springs mineral baths, yoga, meditation, outstanding cuisine, nature walks, and, of course, one massage each day. She read the caption under a picture of two young people in a hot tub:

"Enjoy a relaxing massage under the warm South Carolina sun or beneath the moon and stars in the spa's most private corners. The spa boasts the best facial therapists and massage services in the South and features a full-service beauty salon. A top-of-the-line gym features a cardiovascular area and steam room."

Check-in time was any time after noon on Monday; the first formal meal served would be a light supper on Monday evening, it said, after all the guests had arrived.

Molly decided to leave her car in the garage and take the bus since public transportation had become rather convenient in the wake of skyrocketing gas prices after the last Gulf War. She could walk to the bus stop; the nifty modern suitcases with long handles and rollers made toting a bag hassle-free.

Even though it was the middle of April, the South Carolina weather was warm and sunny with a bright blue sky and a gentle breeze.

She took a walk around the little cottage to make sure all doors, windows, and locks were secure. Then she selected a large-brimmed hat from her ample collection, settled it perfectly on her head in front of the hallway mirror, gathered her trappings, and exited the house. She felt as if a wonderful adventure were about to begin.

3

Molly Arrives at Clareton

It was late evening and dusk had fallen with no ambiguity by the time Molly May reached the bus station in downtown Clareton. It was a small town, and she had some misgivings about finding a cab this late on a Saturday. Her misgivings were short-lived, however, as a cab drove up to the curb before the station door had shut completely behind her as she stepped out onto the sidewalk. The interior of the cab lit up as the driver opened the door and asked her if she needed transportation. As she often reminded her friends, she wasn't afraid of anything – a strange cab in a strange town in the dark of night was no exception; she climbed into the cab without reservation.

"Clareton Manor Wellness Spa, driver," she said briskly. "Do you know where it is?"

"Oh, yes, ma'am, I shore do! Everybody in Clareton knows where Miz Erika's spa is located at. It ain't far, ma'am. We'll be there in a jiffy."

They circled around the downtown square and drove down a broad street with diagonal parking on both sides. It amazed her that such accommodations were still available so close to the overcrowded conditions in Columbia. After a few blocks, the street turned into a highway. By the time the taxicab exited the highway, turning onto a narrow lane with large trees looming on each side, the setting sun had left only a rosy streak across the western sky. As they drove down the lane, Molly gave a casual glance toward the only other house along the way; it was a modest house with a large, old-fashioned rocking-chair porch perched on a hill at the end of steep driveway.

"That's the parson's house, ma'am," the cabbie said, noticing her glance from his mirror. "He must see a lot from up there; by Sunday morning he knows everything that happened in Clareton for the whole week." He chuckled. "Friendly fellow, has a lot of company too."

"Oh, I see. Which church?"

"Sweetwater Fellowship Church. Little white frame church just off the main street downtown. I never been there, of course, but it's well known in town. Well, here we are, ma'am. Clareton Manor. They expecting you?"

As he spoke, the porch light came on, and the front door swung open. "Yes, they are," Molly said as she paid the driver, wishing she could afford a bigger tip. Retrieving her suitcase from the backseat, she headed toward the house where Erika was standing on the porch, waving and calling to her.

Even in the limited porch light, Molly could see that Erika was still as slim as a girl, even as she approached sixty years of age. Her wavy hair seemed brown in most light, but it became auburn in the artificial light; there was only a touch of gray here and there. It was long, but she kept it twisted into a neat figure-eight bun at the nape of her neck. She was fond of wearing long flowing skirts of silk in earth tones, and she was wearing one now. Her fair German complexion contrasted with her auburn hair.

"Wow, Erika!" Molly exclaimed. "What a place!" The Manor House was large and imposing, much larger than Molly had expected. The rising full moon illuminated the impressive façade and the surrounding landscape and revealed dark trails leading off into the woods between hedges of azaleas.

"Do you like it?" Erika laughed her tinkling bell laugh that Molly remembered so well. "It's not paid for!" Her smile was broad, stretching nearly from ear-to-ear.

Molly upended her bag off the wheels and released her grip. A big hug was exchanged.

"How's business?"

"So far, so good. If this week turns out well, I'll be able to cover the monthly bills!"

The Manor was mortgaged to the hilt, as Molly learned over a cup of hot tea with Erika in the kitchen. This would be a make-or-break week for the Spa; everything had to be perfect, and no expense had been spared to ensure that outcome.

"Everything looks great, Erika."

"I've spent a fortune getting things ready for this week. If anyone complains about anything, I'll kill him!"

"Call me first, and I'll help you." They both laughed.

The two old friends talked into the night, laughing over the good times they had shared and expressing their hopes for the future.

It was well past midnight when Molly finally crawled into the most comfortable bed she had ever known. As she rolled over to turn out the lamp by the bed, she noticed on the table by the window a crystal vase of long-stemmed yellow tulips— her favorite. She would explore her lovely room in detail tomorrow, but for now she was exhausted and fell asleep at once.

4

The Rugers from Spartanburg

The shiny, black Mercedes backed out of the four-car garage attached to the 12,000 square foot mansion on High Rock Road in Spartanburg. Purring softly, it turned around in the ample driveway and pulled out into the main thoroughfare.

Abigail, sitting in the front passenger seat, tried to initiate a conversation with her taciturn husband. "Harvey," she said, "I'm so glad you agreed to this vacation. I know a health spa retreat is not exactly your cup of tea, but Marian says it's just the thing to relax and reduce stress. And you have been under a great deal of stress lately, you know."

Harvey shifted his weight uncomfortably in the driver's seat. He had slept late that Monday morning and felt stiff. Normally he was at work by 6:30 in the morning; by now it was after ten, and he was just getting on the road—it made him irritable. Muttering something insignificant in reply to his wife, he steered the powerful motorcar toward the highway.

The Chief Executive Officer of Communications, Inc., in Spartanburg, Harvey Ruger had played all the necessary political games and pulled all the obligatory strings to get where he was. He'd been ruthless, but that was necessary to get where he wanted to go. He was rich, extremely so. But he knew that his business, like many, could be robust one day and fall like a

17

house of cards the next, if the "creative accounting" practices failed or were challenged by the wrong (or right) people. His company's stock had crashed along with the rest of the technical market, but he had known it was coming, his inside information being fairly reliable, and unloaded his shares in time to avoid being caught in the pinch. And his multimillion dollar salary had not been affected so far. The Board of Directors dozed through meetings, content with their six-figure compensation for a half dozen meetings a year. If stockholders had lost money, that was capitalism—the modern version of survival-of-the-fittest, smartest, shrewdest. You pay your money and take your chances; that's the way business worked.

Harvey knew how to win; he wasn't hampered by honesty, integrity or any other old-fashioned values. He was modern, and he knew how the game was played; he didn't make the rules, but he could break them with the best in the business world. Yes, it was stressful, but to him it was worth the fortune he had accumulated. It was harder on his underlings, because they would take the fall if the Securities and Exchange Commission or the State Attorney General got too close. Harvey would insist that as CEO, he was too far removed from the day-to-day activities to be aware of financial details. At 58 years of age he had no intentions of pulling back. Like many others, he had found wealth to be addictive. He wanted to be the wealthiest man in America, even the world, not just another one of hundreds of wealthy men.

The last thing Harvey wanted to do was to spend a week at the Clareton Manor Wellness Spa with his wife, her sister, and that wimpy husband of hers. But he had let himself be cajoled into promising her something special for their thirtieth wedding anniversary, and this is what had come of it. Abigail's sister Marian had read about the new spa in the Living section of the Charleston newspaper and had told Abigail it would be just the thing for her. Marian could not afford it herself, but she said she could enjoy it vicariously through Abigail's description of it if Abigail would only go. So Abigail made up her mind to extract fulfillment of her husband's promise and selected a week at the spa as her anniversary celebration. Then, from her own personal funds, she secretly financed the vacation for her sister and brother-in-law as well; she couldn't bear the thought of spending twenty-four hours a day for a whole week with Harvey alone.

"Marian says they have hot mineral baths, massage therapy and structured exercise programs at the spa. It will be good for you," Abigail promised.

"Exercise! Hmmmph!" Harvey retorted, "Pushing sixty is exercise enough!" He chuckled at his trite joke.

Abby managed a dutiful smile. "Oh, Harvey, you're so clever. Such a dry wit; people always say so." To herself she added, ". . . especially the Corporation lackeys who never think for themselves."

At fifty-one years of age, Abby was still trim and pretty. She looked much younger than her years and worked hard to keep her looks. She was aware that being very feminine and attractive had enabled her to marry a man who was destined for wealth and to have the luxurious lifestyle she enjoyed, and she knew that she had to maintain that persona in order to keep her position.

Inside she felt more like Edith Bunker than a rich society matron, but she tried to conceal her true self except in the presence of her sister Marian and one or two close friends. She did the job she was being paid to do: being the "lady of the house" was her job. She had never loved Harvey, even though there might have been a little infatuation at first—she couldn't remember now; but she had learned to tolerate him. More than a decade had passed since the last beating she suffered at his hands; that event had landed her in the hospital, and it took some skillful public relations work to keep the truth out of the papers. Knowing his career could be ruined if things got out of hand and hit the newspapers, Harvey never took the risk again. Instead he avoided her and spent as much time as possible at the office or his club. They rarely had meals together—only when there were guests—and they had separate luxurious master suites in the huge mansion.

Early in their marriage the beatings had come all too often. She turned her head to the window so Harvey could not see her smile as she remembered those days. Why, even once she had felt so trapped and desperate that the thought of getting rid of Harvey had loomed large in her thoughts. It faded when not only her own sense of morality but also a reluctance to give up her affluent lifestyle took precedence.

She had never forgiven him, though. Somewhere she had read that forgiveness requires two things: That the wrongdoer acknowledge what he did was wrong, and that he tried to make amends based on genuine remorse. Harvey had never done either; if he had a soul, she had never seen any evidence of it.

Her job, at which she excelled, was to be wife, mother, hostess, and trophy. There had been one failure, though, she reminded herself. For all her efforts, their only child, their son Anthony, had not turned out as she hoped, and they saw little of him now that he had dropped out of college and moved to New Orleans. Harvey was bitter in his disappointment in his son and avoided even the mention of his name.

"It will be so nice to see Marian and Francis again. It's been so long," she mused aloud.

Even though Marian and her husband Francis lived in Charleston, a relative short drive from Spartanburg, they rarely visited each other because of the inevitable unpleasantness that arose from Harvey's pompous irascibility.

"Oh, sure, it'll be great," replied Harvey sarcastically.

Abby knew it would be useless to respond.

At this point, quiet returned as the Mercedes sped along the Interstate Highway 26 toward Clareton.

5

The Whitts from Charleston

Heading toward Clareton from Charleston were Marian and Francis Whitt.

Charleston, the grand old lady of the south, with its progressive and tolerant outlook on the earth and its inhabitants along with its kind and genteel manner, was a lovely city.

Born and raised in Charleston, Francis Whitt embodied the spirit of his city. He was a jovial "good ole boy" who generally felt ill will toward no one. His wife Marian had been raised in the Upstate and first visited Charleston when she attended the College of Charleston right out of high school. She fell in love with the city, then later with her Francis, whom she met there. Both their temperaments were good matches for the City's character; they married, settled there, and raised their three children.

Not ambitious like his infamous brother-in-law, Francis had a mediocre job as a government clerk (nowadays, called a "specialist") and made just enough money to support his family in a middle class lifestyle. For most of the years while their children were growing up, Marian, with the homemaking instinct strong in her, had stayed at home to raise the children and make a home for her family, holding only sporadic jobs as a school cafeteria aid or a sitter for the elderly. When the government agency where Francis worked closed and its mission transferred elsewhere, he was offered and accepted the early retirement package. Their income was less than ever, and they restricted their spending to the necessities of life. Since the children were grown and on their own, Francis and Marian had sold the family home and moved to a small, two-bedroom condominium.

Never could they have afforded a week's stay at South Carolina's most luxurious spa, but Marian's older sister Abigail Ruger invited them at her expense. At first both Francis and Marion resisted the offer of charity, but Abby soon made them see that it was for her benefit as much as it was for theirs. "Please rescue me from a monotonous week with my paunchy, bald-headed, egotistical husband," she had pleaded with Marian. Swallowing their discomfort, they agreed.

Marian rarely saw Abby anymore, even though they lived only a half-day's drive apart, because Harvey felt uncomfortable around his impoverished brother-in-law. And Harvey's air of superiority was unpleasant to Francis too, although he tolerated him politely. Actually it had been years since the sisters had seen each other. Their telephone conversations were cordial, if not warm, tinged with only a slight hint of strain.

Arriving ahead of the Rugers, the Whitts drove down the long, shady lane to the front entrance to the Clareton Manor. A young man greeted them, took the car keys, unloaded their luggage from the trunk, and drove the car away. Another young man retrieved the luggage and led them up the wide stone steps and across the portico to the front door.

Marian murmured an agreeable groan as her eyes swept over the tall double doors with an arched transom and side lights of etched, frosted glass. The woods was stained a medium-brown color, but the grain of the wood said mahogany. With a light touch on the door knob by the doorman, the huge door swung inward to reveal a broad expanse of highly polished wood floor accented with a handsome rug in a classic floral design and a curved staircase with a beautifully carved banister. The ceilings must be twelve feet high, at least, Marian thought, as her eyes were drawn upward by the soaring lines in the entry way.

"This is beautiful!" she exclaimed. "It takes my breath away!"

"Not bad," Francis agreed, turning his head from side to side to take it all in.

Peter, acting as doorman, announced the Whitts to Christa, who was doing desk clerk duty, then took them to their spacious room on the second floor. Rather than use the elegant front staircase, they were escorted to the elevator around a corner.

By the time they reached their room, it was mid-morning. After Peter requested their assurance that he could do nothing more for them at the moment, he left them alone.

Marian looked slowly around the room at the tasteful décor. Italian voile curtains with faintly colored peace lilies embroidered into the fabric caught the breeze at the open windows. On the bed there was a matching coverlet and a summer-weight comforter with a 420-thread count (she was sure) duvet. Fresh flowers filled a vase set on a table with a crisp linen tablecloth, trimmed in lace, in front of the east window. The colors were cream, pale yellow, and peach with touches of spring green. The furniture was well-made but not extravagant – probably from China. Polished tables were accented with antique-looking embroidered cloths that Erika had brought from Germany. There was a light, happy feel to the room, with a touch of class.

"Wow," Francis said as he appraised the room. "I haven't seen anything like this since our honeymoon in Paris. Except, of course, your sister's house. But I haven't seen that very often in the past few decades."

"Nice, isn't it?" Marian asked, but it was really a comment, not a question. "I know I'm going to enjoy this week."

"It'll be nice to see Abigail and Harvey again. It's been a long time."

Marian thought she heard a sarcastic edge to Francis's comments. "Let's enjoy these few hours we have before they come," Marian mused aloud; she was anticipating the tension that would probably come in the door with Harvey.

"Sure. What shall we do first?" Francis asked. "How about a walk? I saw an inviting trail headed into the woods we passed on the way in."

"Sounds great to me. Let's stop by the kitchen to see if there's a quick sandwich available."

After changing into their obviously worn sports clothes, they headed off to the kitchen, where they were offered a freshly made tuna salad sandwich (with fresh blackened tuna, not canned) on thinly sliced homemade sourdough bread. After devouring the tasty sandwiches, washed down with lemonade, fragrant with the zest of just-cut lemons, they dashed down the back stairs toward the shady path lined with lavender, pink, and white azaleas. The sun was nearly straight overhead.

6

Unease

By the time dinner was served at seven o'clock in the evening on Monday, all the guests had arrived. It was a diverse group of rich and poor: old money, new money, earned money, inherited money, and working-class near-poverty. In addition to Harvey and Abigail Ruger from Spartanburg, Marian and Francis Whitt from Charleston, and Molly from Columbia, there were Angie and Marcus Bella, a young African-American couple from Raleigh, North Carolina; Dan and Mary Caldwell, an older couple from Petersburg, Virginia; and Nora Pritchard from Atlanta—ten in all.

The large dining room was decorated tastefully without undue ostentation. There was one long table in the center of the room, covered with a white linen tablecloth. The centerpieces consisted of spring flowers: light pink tulips, white asters, blue delphinium, and pale yellow snapdragons. The shadows were lengthening outside, so the diminishing sunlight through several large windows was supplemented with candlelight and a dimmed overhead chandelier. Emanating from an unseen source was the music of Mozart's string quintets.

Erika had carefully thought out the seating arrangement in advance, since she considered interaction with other guests to be an essential part of the spa experience; she was usually very good at it. The head of the table was designated as her place. To her right were place cards for Harvey, Angie, Francis, Nora, and Abigail, in that order. On her left were Marian, Dan, Marcus, Mary, and her old friend Molly at the end of the table, farthest from herself.

As the guests entered the dining room, some of them grimaced at the place cards but took their seats according to Erika's plan. Harvey and Abigail were the last guests to arrive; Harvey's face registered consternation when he realized that he was to be seated next to a "black girl," as he considered her. Abigail saw his hesitation and averted her eyes as she took her place at the end of the table across from Molly.

Molly witnessed the exchange but pretended not to notice. Smiling politely she introduced herself to Abigail. Soon they were exchanging pleasantries about the weather and the accommodations and engaging in other mundane small talk.

During the course of the meal, Molly learned a little about each guest. Dan Caldwell was a retired Lieutenant Colonel, US Army, and had served in Europe, North Africa, and the Orient. He and his wife had the impeccable manners associated with career military members and spouses, learned from the Officer's Handbook on Social Interaction, issued to each new Army officer upon entering the service. In the course of Dan's military career, they had visited spas all over Europe, as well as a few in the Far East. Since retirement they had traveled across the United States to sample various spa experiences; they were delighted that such a fine one had been created so near to their home. They praised the architecture of the Manor House, the food, and the general ambiance. Erika was pleased.

Angie and Marcus Bella were a young African-American couple from Raleigh. They didn't come from "old" money by any means. Life hadn't been easy for them, but they had worked hard and earned Bachelor of Science degrees in computer engineering at North Carolina State University and landed good jobs with high-tech companies at the Research Triangle Park. Just before the stock market bubble burst, they decided to sell the company shares they had received as a sign-on perk to buy a very comfortable house in a fashionable suburb near Raleigh. When the crash came, they were untouched. They had two children whom they adored; the children were staying with grandparents. Obviously enjoying themselves, they seemed not to notice Harvey's rudeness.

Nora Pritchard was an airline executive from Atlanta. She seemed reluctant to divulge any further information about her private life. She admitted to being overdue for a vacation, not having had one in several years. Molly sensed that she seemed ill at ease but her polite questions yielded no clues.

As the meal began, a pleasant dry wine was poured; and by the time the first course was served, the wine had performed its duty and facilitated relaxed light chatter throughout the dining room. Only Harvey sat stiffly detached. Focused on his food, uttering minimal responses to direct questions, he avoided eye contact. Erika tried in vain to engage him in conversation, asking him how his drive down had been ("fine" was all she got in response), asking him about the weather in Spartanburg (again, "fine"), asking him if his room was satisfactory ("yes, fine"). Hiding her exasperation, she left him alone and turned to Marian who was seated on her left.

Marian had pretended not to notice Erika's futile attempts to befriend Harvey, but she understood the process, having been there herself. Harvey did not like to associate with people he considered beneath him, especially women. In contrast to Harvey's distant manner, Marian responded warmly to Erika's overtures: Erika remarked that Charleston had long been one of her favorite cities and lamented that she did not get to visit it as often as she liked. They discussed the tidbits that were being leaked in the news about the upcoming Spoleto; it was something that Marian looked forward to every year.

The meal was served by Erika's son Peter and her daughter Christa, assisted by Chantal and two additional servers. Randy remained in the kitchen, attending to the details on the timing of the meal service. There was a delicate creamed asparagus soup and a salad of fresh greens with a lemony olive oil dressing. After the main course of Circassian Chicken, fresh collard greens, tender baby carrots, baked potato soufflé, and yeast bread hot from the oven, a light dessert of strawberries and cream was served.

Once the last cups and saucers were removed from the table, the guests dispersed to the various diversions prepared for them in the parlor and the screened porch. Marian and Abigail went off to a corner of the parlor to catch up on things since they were last together.

Molly and Erika strolled out onto the front porch and settled into comfortable rocking chairs. The sweet smell of honeysuckle was in the warm air, and a soft breeze whispered through the leaves.

Molly started to rock in her chair. "My, this feels good. Reminds me of being back on the farm when I was young. Nowadays rocking chairs seem to be decorative rather than functional items."

"Too bad too. Rocking promotes circulation of all body fluids; it's a good practice to follow, especially after a large meal."

"You haven't changed a bit, Erika. Everything has to have a health benefit to suit you, doesn't it?"

"Sure, and why not? It's as easy to be well as unwell, you know."

"That's true in these surroundings anyway. Everything is delightful here, Erika. The guest rooms, the dining room, the food, the schedule, the grounds – you've done a wonderful job. I'm happy for you and happy that you invited me to come."

"It's been a lot of hard work, but I love it. So far, so good. Business is growing, and I'm optimistic. But this week is off to a bad start—I'm talking about the tension at the dinner table," Erika noted. "You felt it too, I'm sure. To be honest, my business depends on word-of-mouth recommendations, and I can't afford bad publicity. This week's revenue will keep me out of foreclosure, but . . . I don't know, Molly. It wouldn't take much for things to take a turn for the worse."

Molly could see that Erika was genuinely concerned. "Erika, you're a smart, hard-working businesswoman; you'll succeed. It'll take more than Harvey Ruger's bad manners to derail you. I believe in you."

"And I believe in myself. You're right, Molly. I can't let this get me down. But I do think I may try to have a little talk with Mr. Ruger to see if I can smooth things over."

"Who is he anyway? When I was talking to his wife Abigail at dinner, she mentioned that he was in the communications business but didn't say anything else about what he does for a living."

"You don't know? Harvey Ruger is the CEO of Communications, Inc. in Spartanburg. Surely you've heard of him; he's been in the papers—a lot lately, I might add."

"Oh, yes, now I remember. There's been some talk of a possible investigation by the Securities and Exchange Commission, hasn't there? Some stockholders are wondering why the stock dropped so far so fast. Luckily I didn't own any of it!"

"I wouldn't want any of the guests or staff to know it, but I did own it. I bought a few shares many years ago; after multiple splits, the price continued to soar and I sold it all to make a down payment on this place. There wasn't any insight on my part; the timing was coincidental, but I made usurious return on my investment and got out before the crash. I suppose you could say Harvey and his company are responsible for my being able to establish Clareton Manor Spa. It was just a start, though, and I've mortgaged it to the maximum to bring it to the standard you see here."

"Whew. What a coincidence. No one knows?"

"No one. Not even Peter and Christa. I think it's best that they don't know. Besides, one of my employees wasn't so fortunate."

"Who?"

"Barry Kholer. He's a massage therapist from town who works here for me when there are resident guests at the spa. He's an excellent therapist. He and Peter have become friends, and after a couple of glasses of wine one night, he told him the whole story of how Communications, Inc. took him from rags to riches, so to speak." According to Peter, deep down he's still bitter about the collapse of the company stock. He holds a grudge against the company management."

"Including Harvey Ruger."

"Especially Harvey."

"As you always said, Erika, no matter how much we protest, in some way we're responsible for everything that happens to us. None of us likes to be cheated, but sometimes we can be too gullible."

Erika smiled her wide smile and her eyes twinkled as she looked at her old friend. "Yes, we did have those discussions many years ago, didn't we?"

"Those and many like them. Does Barry know who Mr. Ruger is?"

"Could it be possible that he doesn't? Certainly he must. And he knows that he has an appointment with Mr. Ruger for a massage tomorrow afternoon. He hasn't asked to switch with Christa, so he must intend to do his job. He's a professional; I have confidence that he will conduct himself as one tomorrow."

"You don't sound so sure about that. I know what a good judge of character you are, so if you have misgivings, there must be a reason."

"Maybe it's just a touch of anxiety about everyone having a good time this week. I'm concerned about the Bellas. How can they enjoy the week with Harvey's obvious antagonism? If I can't come to some understanding with Harvey, I may just have to try to keep them apart."

"That won't be easy with such a small group of guests."

"I'll do the best I can and hope things turn out all right. What else can I do?"

"Whatever you do will be the right thing," Molly said in her most soothing voice.

Soon the only sound was the rhythmic crunching of the rockers of their chairs on the porch as the two old friends relaxed into the peace of the cool Southern evening.

7

It's Not Okay

Taking leave early in the evening after dinner, Angie and Marcus Bella returned to their room. As soon as the door was closed behind them, Marcus let out what he could hold in no longer. "I didn't think that kind of bigotry existed any more!" he boomed. He was referring to Harvey Ruger's rude behavior to him and especially to his wife, next to whom he was seated at dinner. "He barely spoke to you!"

"He didn't speak to me at all," Angie corrected. "You know it makes me angry too, but there's nothing to be gained by indulging ourselves in thoughts of retribution. Let's just enjoy our vacation. There's so much to do here, and we've paid enough for it, that's for sure."

"How can we enjoy it with that buffoon frowning all over us? I'd like to bop him one! Call him outside and bop him just once!"

"Hush, Marcus! Don't even talk like that! Didn't that thirty days you spent in jail ten years ago teach you that when you punch someone, you get the worst of it?"

She was referring to an incident when Marcus was still a teenager, just out of high school, in which he became involved in an altercation at a club one Saturday night. Too much alcohol combined with too much testosterone and insults had escalated

33

to punches. Marcus landed a lucky one that sent one bully to the hospital and Marcus to the county jail. The victim recovered fully except for a scar to his ego.

Marcus looked at it as just one of those things that should not have happened but somehow did anyway. "Come on, Angie. Don't preach. You know I'm just letting off steam. But somehow, someday, those guys have got to learn that they aren't the lords of the plantation anymore. My money's as good as his, and my blood's as red as his, and I can prove it."

"I'm sure you can, honey, but please don't try," Angie teased him, as she patted and pinched his arm.

"Okay, babe. I won't." He laughed and relaxed a little with her teasing. He adored her; she was good for him.

They were a good-looking couple. Marcus was short and stocky, and the extra weight he carried hid the well-developed muscles underneath. Angie was slightly taller than Marcus and had a natural Barbie Doll figure. Although her face was plain and she wore little makeup, that figure attracted the men at work like the proverbial flies to honey. She was always polite and occasionally flirted a little, but Marcus was her soul mate and they both knew it.

With a good education, resulting in good jobs, they were able to live middle class lives in a middle class neighborhood. The poor side of town, where they had grown up and where trouble of one sort or another always lurked around the next corner, seemed far away to them now. Those days were all but forgotten.

When Marcus calmed down, Angie went to the telephone and dialed her mother's number. "I want to speak to the children; I miss them," she explained to Marcus as the phone rang at the other end.

"Tell them I said hello, and I love them. Your mother too. I'm going to the gym and stretch out a little bit—get rid of this tension." He put on his gray sweatpants and a matching t-shirt. Throwing a towel across his shoulders, he sauntered out the door. "I'll be back in half an hour, Angie," he called out as he left.

"Okay, Marcus. Tomorrow maybe I'll join you, but tonight, I'm going to talk to the kids, then take a long lavender bath and read a magazine."

After a good chat on the phone, she locked the door and went to the bathroom to turn on the faucet. Soon the room was steamy, and she settled down for a good soak.

8
New Orleans

"No! No! No! I won't go with you, and that is my final answer!" exclaimed Cindy. "I won't be involved in anything that could get too close to crossing the line. And you know I won't, Tony, so you can stop asking me. I told you that from the start; I won't do it!"

"But it's my own home," Tony cajoled. "Mom and Dad won't mind at all. You know Mom gives me anything I ask for and always has. I won't take anything that isn't mine. I left some things at Mom and Dad's house that I need. Like my leather jacket. It would have been nice this past winter."

"Then why don't you go when they are at home, instead of waiting until they are away on vacation?"

"I've told you how Dad feels about me. He doesn't want to see me. If I go when he is at home, there could be a scene. I don't want to go through that again."

Tony crossed the room and stood looking out the second-story window at the passersby on the dirty back street in New Orleans. Tony Ruger had been born into a wealthy family, but now he lived in a small flat with his latest girlfriend Cindy Celina. He had received a brief note from his mother telling him that she and his father were taking a vacation from their home in Spartanburg to a new health spa in the midlands of South Carolina. They would be gone nearly a week. Tony immediately seized upon it as a perfect opportunity to return to his family home and scout around for some items he had left behind in his haste to leave. He wanted Cindy to go with him, but she suspected that he had other motives as well.

Turning away from the window, Tony began stowing a few items into his suitcase. "Cindy, please. I need to have you with me. I don't want to go back there and face the memories alone. I need you. Please." His dark eyes pleaded with her, and his mournful expression touched her heart. He had a self-assured, confident manner that was useful in winning others over to his point of view.

She hesitated, took a deep breath, and let out a slow sigh. "Well, okay. I will go with you. But if you so much as look sideways at the silver service or a chunk of jewelry, I'm calling 911. I mean it. You know I mean it. I'm not a crook, and I won't be involved in a burglary with you. Understand?"

"Sure I do. Don't worry. Trust me!"

Cindy went to the closet and pulled out her own suitcase, put it on the bed, opened it, and turned toward the closet.

Slim and fit, she wore her clothes like a model. At twenty-one, she was five years younger than Tony and had been attracted by his self-assured manner and good looks. He had wavy black hair and dimples that showed when he talked or smiled. He had a quick laugh and enjoyed life. However, he was a little too happy-go-lucky and lacked the talent for holding a job. He lived mainly on the allowance his mother continued to send him, even after he dropped out of college. For that matter, neither of them had a job at the time.

After packing, they loaded the car and set off on the twelve-hour drive to Spartanburg. The sun was just setting in the west, and they turned east onto Highway 10 toward Mobile. They hadn't gone far when the traffic slowed to a crawl, then stopped.

Tony remembered one of his father's cynical maxims: "If you don't think you have any influence on other people in this world, try crashing your car on the freeway at rush hour."

Apparently someone had done just that. After forty minutes of inching along, they were finally on their way again. They would arrive before sunrise. Good, Tony thought. That would mean they probably would not be seen on the winding road to the mansion at the end of High Rock Road.

9

Barry's Predicament

Standing in front of his mirror, Barry Kholer admired himself—dressed in a stylish dark suit with a perfectly matching tie, a modern one with pattern and color but subtle enough not to be obvious. He liked the way he felt when he was dressed well. He tilted his head to one side to get a better look at his hair; yes, a proper haircut. Not easy to get nowadays, even for top dollar. He'd been to four, no, five, hair stylists before he'd achieved the look he desired. Not that he could afford it anymore.

After completing training for his massage therapists license about a year ago, he had snagged a part-time job at the Clareton Manor Wellness Spa. He couldn't believe getting a relatively menial job made him feel lucky. After all, he had been an up-and-coming stockbroker and had made quite a lot of money for himself as well as for his clients. Unfortunately, he had overinvested in Communications, Inc., and when its stock dropped to less than twenty-five percent of it peak value, Barry found himself in a very unpleasant impecunious state. His clients dropped him; his boss fired him. Nothing was yet proven, and there had been no indictments, but the CEO of Communications, Inc., and the upper echelon of its managers were the only ones who came out ahead. As these thoughts floated through his mind, Barry felt the anger reverberate in his belly.

When he was well-to-do, Barry had been accustomed to the finer things in life, including weekly massages for himself. Searching for a temporary income to tide him over while he was looking for a new job, he decided that he could get by as a massage therapist until something more lucrative opened up. He attended a local school in Augusta, and during classroom exercises, he was praised by his classmates for his strength and skill. It wasn't his idea of an elegant occupation, but with demand increasing by the day, it paid the rent.

Taking off his suit—which he never wore much anymore— Barry turned his attention to getting ready for work. Erika's latest spa week had begun the day before, and he had a full schedule of clients for today. Erika paid him a salary, but his primary income came from the spa clients themselves who were always wealthy and usually generous tippers. The more relaxed and happy they became during the week; the bigger the tips. Still the capitalist at heart, Barry admitted to himself only that his apparent devotion to his client's well-being was really his own devotion to his pocketbook.

Dressed in dark, loose-fitting sports pants and a white cotton knit shirt with a V-neck and long sleeves with fitted cuffs, his sleek build was visible beneath the soft fabric. At least, he thought, admiring himself in the mirror, this kind of work makes it easy to stay in shape.

He stepped outside into the bright morning sunlight and headed for his motorcycle parked at the street. It was nearly eight-thirty, and his first appointment was at nine. He would have to hurry.

The massage therapy suite at the Clareton Manor Wellness Spa consisted of two separate rooms. Both he and Christa Bischoff were nationally certified massage therapists; and each had a room for clients. With ten guests at the spa, each of them would normally be assigned five clients a day. However, in South Carolina, massage therapy was still not recognized as a health or wellness treatment; therefore, it was illegal for a therapist to treat a client of a different gender. As a result, Barry treated the four male guests, and Christa the six female guests.

Barry liked the arrangement, assuming that men were generally bigger tippers. Even though he could have made more money by being on his own—he received only a percentage of the fee here—he liked having the Spa staff take care of the tedious chores of laundry and tidying the room. Besides the tips were better here.

When he arrived at Clareton Manor, he parked his motorcycle around back. Walking quickly up the back steps, he glanced at his watch and saw that he had just enough time to get the room set up before his first client was due. After washing up, he went to the therapy room and picked out music to play on the stereo. Then he clicked on the portable electric heater and dimmed the lights.

His first client of the day was Dan Caldwell, an elderly man with wrinkled skin, which made it a little more difficult because the skin tended to fold over as the muscles were kneaded. Dan was a gentleman, kind and polite. Having had many massages over his lifetime, he immediately began the slow, even, deep breathing required for a satisfactory treatment without prompting by Barry. Conversation was limited to basic introductions and a general medical evaluation at the start and later to that necessary for the treatment.

Dan Caldwell's wife Mary was next door with Christa. When they had both finished, they met in the hallway outside. Mary smiled broadly at Christa and said, "Thank you," then turned to Dan. "Christa's great," she said. "How was your massage?"

"Wow," said Dan. "Barry did a great job too. He's at least as good as the best therapist I've suffered under before—better than most. I think I'm going to enjoy this week at Clareton Manor."

"Me too. I can hardly wait for tomorrow to do that again." Mary laughed. "It takes a lot of strength to do that kind of work all day."

"You know what?" said Dan, as they walked toward their room. "Barry Kohler told me that he used to be a stockbroker! Lost too much money for his clients and got himself fired. Said he used to be a wimp. Said he has to work out to stay in shape to do this job. Said Peter Bischoff was his personal trainer and a good one—suggested we sign up for a session or two with Peter while we're here. I think I'll give it a try later. Want to go with me?"

"Maybe tomorrow. For me today it's going to be a ten minute walk in the sunshine. I need my Vitamin D."

Barry watched them walk down the hall. It was only ten-oh-five; he had nearly a thirty minute break before his next client. "Time for a 'smoke' break, Christa?" he laughed. He had quit smoking a year ago, but he hadn't broken the habit of stepping outside at break time.

Christa laughed and joined him.

They walked down a rather long, narrow hall to an exit used by only the staff. They stepped out onto the stoop. Randy was coming up the path from his cottage; they waved to him as he passed by the Manor on one side, heading toward the kitchen entrance.

"What's for lunch?" Christa called out. "Hey, didn't I just see you in the kitchen?"

"American potluck surprise," Randy called back flippantly as he rounded the corner. He generally didn't disclose his menus ahead of time. Christa's other question went unanswered.

Turning back to Barry, Christa initiated some small talk about how their first appointments of the day had gone. "When Mom first started out in this business when I was just a kid, she earned hardly enough to make ends meet. Few people in this country, and particularly in the south, knew what to think of a massage in those days. But the popularity of massage therapy has grown so much that there's enough work for anyone who wants to get into it."

Barry responded, "It's a growing craze; that's certain. It's hard work, but it pays the rent. And I have to admit I enjoy helping people enjoy life. It's better than being some corrupt corporate CEO who throws working people into poverty without a second thought."

"You're thinking about Harvey Ruger, now, aren't you?" asked Christa.

"Yes, I am. He has an appointment with me this afternoon at three o'clock."

"How do you feel about that?"

"I feel okay. I've learned a difficult lesson, but I think I finally understand that I should not do unto others things that I don't want done to me. I'm going to do the best job I can possibly do. Maybe kindness will soften him up."

"You're okay, Barry. Good luck."

"Thanks. I'll need it."

A slight shiver of unease flashed down Christa's spine, as she turned back toward the Manor House to resume her duties. Barry seemed a little too casual, a little insincere. Oh, well, she thought, if I had lost my entire way of life because of unethical, if not illegal, activities by a man who will probably never see justice, I would probably feel the same way Barry does.

Part II

Where's Harvey?

10
Tony Plans His Caper

The full moon still brightened the night but was fading with the dawn as Tony and Cindy took exit 72A off Interstate 85. At the bottom of the ramp the car took a right and sped off through the winding thoroughfares of Spartanburg's best neighborhoods, turning several times before reaching the High Rock Road signpost. There was very little traffic; they had seen only two cars and a delivery truck during the last few miles of their journey. Making the familiar turn onto High Rock Road, Tony felt calm and confident. Stillness prevailed except for the smooth movement of the single car on the street; no one had paid any special attention to them, he was sure.

At last he reached the driveway to his parents' mansion. The design and construction of the cement was so precise that he did not feel the usual jarring and bouncing of the car shocks as he turned. What a joint! he thought as he steered the car to the rear of the house and parked in the shadows cast by the trees and house. Even though he had once called it home, it was hard for him to comprehend that some people lived in such affluence, while others lived in discarded refrigerator boxes. "Here we are at last," Tony said softly as he heaved a sigh.

49

"I'm so glad; I'm tired." Cindy opened the car door and stretched her long legs with a relieved groan. Then she opened her eyes fully and looked up at the massive structure in front of them.

"Wow!" she said. "You ran away from this? This is what I'd call 'opulent,' and I don't use that word lightly!"

"I don't need it, sweetie; I've got you!" And he put his arm around her shoulders and hugged her to him.

She gave him a sideways glance and a crooked smile. "Okay, Mister Altruism, let's get this over with."

It had been over twelve hours since they had left New Orleans with stops just for gas and a quick bite to eat. Her fatigue overcame her apprehension at entering the unoccupied house. "Let's go in," she said. "I'd like to stretch out on the floor and get some real sleep."

"Let's go then," Tony responded. He got out of the car, fumbling for the right key in the dim light of dawn as he headed for the back door. The third one he tried inserted smoothly into the keyhole and turned. "The third one's the charm," he muttered absentmindedly. To Cindy, he said, "At least they didn't have the locks changed. Mom still wants me to feel at home here and to come whenever I want."

"Don't you think she'd prefer if you came when she was at home?" Cindy was still chiding him about what she considered to be an unauthorized intrusion.

"Sure. But I'll see her soon enough, I'm sure. I'll tell her about our visit then."

As the door swung open, he stood aside and let Cindy enter in front of him. There were lights on somewhere in the house, probably in one of the master bedroom suites and the main sitting room; both may be on timers, he thought. With that light, together with the first glow of dawn streaming in the east windows, they could see well enough without flicking on a switch. Everything was just as he remembered it except for the accessories; his mom changed those nearly once a month.

"Make yourself at home, Cin; I'll get the luggage."

"Yeah, right." In spite of her apprehension at being in the mansion uninvited, she couldn't resist a look around. She had never been in a house like this. She searched for the bathroom; there were several, and the one she chose was bigger than their apartment in New Orleans.

Meanwhile Tony was reaching into the trunk of the car; he retrieved their two small overnight bags. He looked around as he closed the trunk lid. Nothing was amiss. Just as he turned toward the back door of the house, Tony thought he saw a flicker of light in the woods, but as he swung around to check, it was gone. Just nerves, he thought. Natural.

Meeting him at the door, Cindy quipped, "Nice place you got here, old friend." He put down the luggage on the kitchen floor.

"It's spotless, even under the chair legs."

"Well, Mom has help, of course."

"Help? Isn't that southern dialect for 'underpaid hired servants'?"

He wrapped his arms around her and gave a little squeeze. "The resulting labor cost savings helps to defray the expense of the errant son," he teased.

"Not to mention his latest girlfriend," she added.

"Let's grab a quick nap and be on our way."

"I'm up for that."

After a few hours sound sleep, they awakened to bright sunlight. As Cindy put together a light breakfast from the supplies she found in the pantry and refrigerator, Tony headed upstairs to his old room, which his mother had kept the same as it was when he lived there. He searched the closet and dresser drawers, finding nothing that he wanted to take with him. Clothes more than a year old were clearly out of style. His poor man's pride wouldn't let him wear them.

Listening to make sure Cindy was still bustling about the kitchen, banging pans with utensils, he turned toward his father's master suite. As noiselessly as possible, he slowly opened the door and slipped inside, pushing the door nearly closed behind him. Quickly he set to work to find what he knew must be there. He slid his hands under folded shirts in the drawers and opened lids to carved, wooden boxes.

His hands did not find the object of their search. Now where . . . Tony thought. Maybe in the safe? He knew where the safe was, behind an old-fashioned hinged picture. He swung the picture away from the wall; then he tried the combination that he remembered from watching his father as a child, but it did not work. Of course, his dad would have changed it, Tony chided himself.

The room was shadowy because of its location on the west side of the house and the heavy draperies nearly covering the windows. Where would his father keep the combination to the safe? Not just in his head; Tony was sure of that. Harvey would have a back up plan in case he forgot the numbers. Surely he would have a copy of it in his safe deposit box at the bank—they could make a quick run to the bank as soon as it opened and be back in no time. He knew he could talk Cindy into anything; she was smart and sensitive, but she loved him too much for her own good. Love can make even smart people do dumb things sometimes.

A subsequent search in all the likely spots for the safe deposit box key also turned up nothing; his father must have it with him. His thoughts raced ahead. After coming this far, he could not lose this opportunity; he would *have* to get the key. If that meant driving on to Clareton, which was not that far after all, and searching for the key in his father's room at the spa, he would do it. Harvey would not be able to keep the key with him always at the spa; there would be the hot mineral baths, the massage therapy, the exercise room, where one did not take keys.

He went downstairs and breezed into the kitchen with a big smile. "Breakfast smells great!" he exclaimed as he sat down on a stool at the granite-topped counter.

"Did you find your things?" asked Cindy.

"Well, not exactly," replied Tony, forkfull of scrambled egg in one hand and a piece of crunchy buttered toast aimed at his mouth in the other.

"Not exactly? Clarify, *mon vieux*."

"You've been living in New Orleans for six months now, and you've already started picking up the lingo."

"Seven months. What do you mean, 'not exactly'?" she persisted.

"One of the closets is locked, and I think my leather jacket is in there. I couldn't find the key to the closet; it may be in the safe." Tony amazed himself sometimes at how quickly he could come up with a semi-plausible lie.

"In the safe! Tony, don't you *think* about opening the safe! They'll know someone has been here! I won't be an accomplice to burglary—not even for you. I told you that!"

"Relax, Cindy. Don't worry. I can't open the safe; I don't have the combination."

Cindy didn't relax; the creases in her forehead indicated that she was worried. "Then let's just have breakfast, erase our trail, and head back to New Orleans." She was starting to feel the stress more intensely; she remembered reading in one of Harold Kushner's books that being pressured into compromising one's values could be more stressful than anything else. At the moment, she heard its ring of truth. "What do you say?" she wheedled.

Letting out a clipped sigh, Tony grasped the back of a kitchen chair and turned to look at her straight on. "No, Cindy. I can't do that. It would be foolish to come this far and then just leave without what I came for, wouldn't it? I want my leather jacket. You know I could have put it to good use this past winter. I think I may know where dear ole Popsy keeps a copy of the combination, and I'm going to look for it."

Cindy felt like crying. What had she gotten herself into? The sudden stern tone in Tony's voice startled and frightened her. She turned away, her long hair hiding her face from him. "What are you going to do?"

"I'm almost sure Dad must keep a copy of the combination somewhere—he wouldn't trust his memory. He always likes a back up plan."

"Where?"

"Probably in the safe deposit box at the bank."

"What good does that do you? You can't get in the safe deposit box, can you?" Cindy sounded resigned in spite of her sarcasm. She had run through a list of her options in her mind, and the list had only one item on it. She was stuck. She had no money. She had no way home except with Tony.

"No."

"Then, what . . . what . . ." Cindy faltered as she realized what Tony was prepared to do.

"Look, Cindy, if you really don't want to go with me, you can stay here. I'll be back in a few hours. By night anyway."

"Here! I can't stay here! Someone would surely catch me. The maids or the gardeners. Where are you going?"

"To Clareton. I'm going to Clareton to the spa and get the key from my father."

"But I thought you said you didn't want to see him. Surely you don't think he will give it to you? Why not just ask for the key to the closet and get your jacket"

"I'm not going to *ask* him for the key; I'm just going to borrow it. I won't see him, and he won't see me. He'll have to undress for the hot springs and the massage therapy. I'll just take the key out of his pocket while he's out of the room."

"You're nuts."

"No, I'm not. It'll be easy. Cindy, you worry too much. You know that, don't you? You have to take some risks in life in order to feel alive. A little excitement to get the adrenalin flowing."

"Can't you come up with an alternative? It sounds crazy to take such a big risk for nothing more than a leather jacket.

Your mother will send you money to buy a new one, if you only ask her."

"I want *that* jacket." Tony was beginning to lose patience, something he rarely did. "Let's clean up the kitchen. We don't have time to run the dishwasher, so we'll just wash up by hand, the old-fashioned way. Here put these on," he added, handing her a pair of kitchen vinyl gloves. "No dishpan hands for my angel."

Back upstairs, he carefully wiped off everything he had touched. He did not want to leave any traces. As they prepared to leave, they checked and doubled-checked to make sure things were left just as they had found them. As they exited the back door, Tony wiped the door knobs clean.

11
Tony Visits the Manor

Neither Tony nor Cindy noticed the man sitting on the porch of the house located to their right just after they turned off the main road onto the lane leading to Clareton Manor Spa.

Tony stopped the car in a grove of trees a good half mile down the lane from the main building but well out of sight of the single house he had passed on the way in. He turned the little blue Toyota around, facing toward the main road to save time on his way out, in case he needed it, getting so close to the trees that the branches raked against Cindy's window. Taking out his cell phone and flicking it open, he dialed the number for the Clareton Manor Wellness Spa that he had looked up while in Spartanburg and committed to memory.

"Good afternoon, Clareton Manor," came a cheery voice in response to two short rings.

"Oh, hello. I was wondering if you could tell me the number of the room in which Mr. and Mrs. Ruger are staying?" Tony tried to sound businesslike. He hoped they did not have caller ID, but even if they did, cell phones were still not easy to trace.

"Room 7, sir. May I connect you?"

"Yes, please." If anyone answered, Tony would just hang up. After five or six rings, the pleasant clerk came back on the

57

line. "Mr. and Mrs. Ruger are not in at the moment. Would you like to leave a message?"

"No, I think not. Perhaps I'll call back later. What time do you suppose they might be in?"

"I'll check my schedule, sir." And after a brief pause, "Mr. Ruger has a massage therapy session scheduled until four-thirty. And I do believe I see Mrs. Ruger in the parlor at a bridge table. Shall I call her for you?"

"No, no. I would never dare to interrupt her bridge game!" Tony said, laughing. "It was really Mr. Ruger I wanted to speak with. I'll call back after four-thirty. You've been very helpful. Thank you very much. Good-bye."

Tony ended the call and closed the telephone with a snap. With a broad smile, Tony turned to Cindy and exclaimed, "Perfect! Things are falling into place—they're both out of the room and engaged in activities that will distract them for an hour at least." Then, getting out of the car, he added, "I'll be back in ten minutes. Cheer up, kid!"

Cindy sat frozen in the car and did not answer.

Tony sneaked toward the big house, using the copse along the driveway for cover. After every few steps, he stopped to search as far as he could see on all sides—he saw no one. Once he reached the house, he kept very close to it and concealed himself behind the landscaping when he could. He made it to the back of the house and entered through what looked like an employee's entrance; he took a left and soon found himself at the end of the long guest-room wing. Carpeted steps led to the second floor.

Mentally calculating that a spa this size would probably have no more than ten guest rooms, the lower room numbers on the first floor and Number Five through Ten upstairs, Tony started up the stairs. At the top of the stairs he turned a corner, checking the numbers on the doors. Just then a door opened and out stepped a tall, slim, pinched-looking woman of about fifty; he made a quick decision to "hide in the open," so to speak, and pose as one of the staff. He smiled and wished her a good day. She made a terse response but did not acknowledge him with a glance.

Without pausing, he continued briskly on, turned the corner at the end of the hall and waited until he was sure she was out of sight. Then he reversed his steps until he reached Number Seven. He knocked lightly; there was no answer. He gently turned the knob; it was locked. Now for the old credit card trick, he thought, and retrieved a card from his wallet. He slid the card between the door and the jamb, and the simple latch fell open. Looking both ways and seeing no one, he stepped inside and quickly shut the door behind him.

He had to work fast. His eyes darted over the room, looking for a ring of keys. None were on the dresser top; he opened the top drawer. There they were! He sorted through the keys and found only two that had the familiar shape and style of safe deposit box keys and removed one of them from the ring. His breath felt heavy, and his heart was beating hard.

Suddenly, there were footsteps in the hall! Jamming the key ring back into the drawer and sliding it shut, he made two long steps to the closet and tucked himself behind the door, just as the door to the room was opening. Through the crack in the door, he watched as the form emerged—it was Harvey! Tony held his breath.

At first Harvey headed for the private bathroom, but then he detoured and stopped at the dresser. The top drawer was not quite shut tight. He placed his hand on the drawer handle and drew it out, glanced in the drawer, grabbed a package of cigarettes from the drawer and picked up the telephone.

Lighting a cigarette, he dialed a number from memory. After a brief pause, he said into the receiver, "Hello, Lillie? This is Mr. Ruger. Any messages for me today?" Then his father said, "Well, look, tell him I'll see him tomorrow afternoon. Make an appointment for about 5:30, will you? This place is getting on my nerves. I'll leave Mrs. Ruger here and head home tomorrow afternoon. I should be there in plenty of time." With that, he hung up the phone and went directly to the bathroom.

By the time he opened the door and slid into the driver's seat, Tony was panting. He didn't turn to look at Cindy, but she was scrutinizing his face for clues. Wasting no time, he started the car and drove back down the lane toward the main road.

Reverend Stromb was still sitting on the porch, only slightly less focused than he had been a half hour before. This time he noticed a dark-haired young man driving the blue Japanese car, and it seemed to be going a little faster than before. After the car passed out of sight, he returned to his rocking and sipping. Odd, he thought.

"Tony! Tony!" cried Cindy. "What happened? Tell me. Tell me quick! Tell me nothing went wrong!"

"Oh, Cindy," replied Tony, trying to sound exasperated. "You do worry too much, you know. Everything went fine. Dad was out of the room, having his massage. I went in, found the keys in the top dresser drawer, took one off the key ring, and came back to the car. That's all!" He didn't mention that his father planned to return to Spartanburg the next day.

"No one saw you?" Cindy was skeptical.

"No one. Well, no one important anyway. I did pass one old lady in the hall and wished her a pleasant 'good day.' I don't think she even looked at me, and if she did, she just thought I was part of the staff. No, everything went great. Just great. Couldn't have been better!" Thinking about the smooth, numbered key in his pocket, he turned to Cindy and gave her a big dimpled smile. He was beginning to relax a little.

His thoughts were elsewhere. Time was important now. His Dad would eventually realize that the safe deposit box key was missing, and he could certainly call the bank. Tony needed to get what he was after and plant the key back in his parent's home—or not, he was not sure of the best disposal plan at this point.

He took the state road up to Ninety-Six and then crossed over to the Interstate. It was a one-hundred mile trip back to Spartanburg; Tony made it in about one and one quarter hours. He knew where the bank was and drove straight there. It was nearing five o'clock, closing time for the bank.

Cindy sighed with relief when the car finally stopped. High speeds made her uncomfortable, to say the least. "Do you really think they will let you access your father's safe deposit box? Surely they know him by sight!"

"Oh, come on, Cindy. Does your bank teller know you? Now'days, tellers don't recognize customers at all. The big banks have merged into mega-banks and management has decided that it's more cost-effective to hire temporary, part-time roving tellers who go from bank-to-bank, working a day here and a day there. At the low wages they pay, the turnover is high. The temp tellers never get to know the clientele. Even the big shots, like my dear old dad. Wish me luck," he added over his shoulder as he got out of the car, taking his small leather briefcase with him. It was cowhide; he couldn't abide the pigskin that was turning up everywhere these days—made in China.

"Good luck," Cindy replied. She looked around, as if trying to identify a likely escape route for herself if anything seemed amiss while Tony was inside completing his transaction. "I'm not this kind of girl, you know."

Tony entered the bank and stopped at the receptionist's desk. "Good afternoon. I'd like to access my safe deposit box please," he said pleasantly.

"Certainly," she replied. "Right this way." She walked over to the vault area and stopped at the card file outside. "Name?" she asked.

"Ruger," he stated calmly with his usual pleasant, dimpled smile, looking her directly in the eye.

The clerk fumbled with the file and finally pulled out a card. "Excuse me, please," she said, " but this is the first time

I've had to get a safe deposit box for someone at this bank, and I'm not sure of the procedure. I'll have to ask one of the others. Wait here, and I'll be right back."

As she turned her back and walked toward the teller corral, Tony felt panic hit him. Was she on to him? Did she know his dad? He felt sure there was only one Ruger in the file. Should he sneak out the back door? "Whoa, slow down, pal," he said to himself. "Isn't that what I just said? A new clerk who doesn't know her job and certainly doesn't know 'Mr. Ruger.'" He decided to take his chances; running from the bank if there was no problem would no doubt draw suspicion to him. He took a deep breath and smiled his affable smile. I can handle this, he thought. After all, his charm had never failed him before.

In a few minutes, the clerk returned and said, "Okay, I think I've got it now. Just initial here please." He did as he was told, copying the previous initials of his father as closely as possible. He deliberately garbled the date in order to distort its value as evidence, if it ever came to that.

Soon, the vault door was open, two keys in the box turned after several tries, and the door opened. "Just let me know when you're finished," the clerk said as she left him alone. Tony felt relief at the realization that he had gotten this far; his father had not yet discovered that a key was missing and called the bank.

Tony pulled open the box and set it down on the table provided in the gated room. It was a large box, heavy with all sorts of documents and boxes and bags. He was tempted to check the will but changed his mind. The future would take care of itself; he had to keep the time in the vault to the absolute minimum for now. He just needed the combination to the safe. As he was sorting through the papers, his hands pressed against some bags. He stopped to feel the bags to guess their contents. It felt like the shape of coins; he opened the bag. There they were: the gold coins he hoped to find in the safe at the house.

Dozens of them. Worth at least half a million in today's market, he was sure. He closed the bag and inserted it deftly into his briefcase. He closed the safe deposit box, returned it to its cubicle, turned the key, and exited the vault.

So the coins had been in the safe deposit box, not the safe, as he believed. And there were many, many more than he had guessed. He wondered if he should have taken just a few—maybe then they would not be missed right away. But, no, he was sure his dad counted them frequently; he had always enjoyed that sort of thing. He would be as easily caught taking a few as he would if he took them all. If you're going to sell your soul, he thought, make sure you get a good price for it.

He waved at the receptionist to tell her he was leaving. She saw him, smiled and nodded in acknowledgment.

Out the door he went. He'd pulled it off! He could hardly believe it. Now, all he had to do was to dispense with the loot before anyone discovered it was missing. There would be no way anyone could trace it to him.

Cindy was startled when she saw the door open and Tony emerge. She half expected—no, she totally expected—him to be in police custody by now.

Tony opened the car door and dropped the briefcase on the floor of the backseat. It fell with a heavy thud. "Mission accomplished," he said. "As soon as we get this key back home, we can head back to New Orleans."

It wasn't far to the big house on High Rock Road. Tony was a little concerned about being seen there in daylight, but he had no choice. Deciding that it would be hard to explain how the key got out of the house and then back in, Tony tossed it into a flower bed by the back door where it would be easy to find, presuming that a scenario in which someone (maybe a prowler?) found it there, used it, and returned it, would be plausible in a stretch.

Cindy waited in the car. Noticing that he came back without going into the house and without the leather jacket he claimed as the purpose of this whole escapade, Cindy started to ask about it, but she knew there were things going on that she did not want to know. She felt that she was in too deeply already. She remained silent as they drove away.

12
Where Is Harvey?

Tuesday morning at Clareton Manor broke bright and sunny; the moods of the spa guests matched the weather, except for one. Upon rising and readying for the day, Abigail did not fail to notice that Harvey Ruger was his usual grumpy self. He mentioned to her that he had had a call from the office and might have to go back for a few hours to straighten some things out. She didn't argue with him. He was still in the bathroom when she called out to him that she was going downstairs.

Around the breakfast table, the enthusiastic chatter of Erika outlined the day's activities and options. Harvey's seat was notably empty; he had ordered breakfast sent to his room. His absence added to the lightness of the mood.

Soon, everyone was off, signing up for various activities for the day and week, and lining up for their chosen activities. The morning passed amiably.

After lunch, there was a yoga practice, followed by image-guided meditation, led by an eastern-trained instructor from Columbia. Everyone attended, again except Harvey. He had scheduled his afternoon massage at three o'clock in the afternoon, deliberately avoiding the "mumbo jumbo," as he called it. At first Abigail thought he might have gone to

Spartanburg as he said he might, but when she passed by the window on the north side of the library, she noticed the black Mercedes was still in the parking lot.

By four o'clock the scheduled events were over, and free time remained before dinner. Angie and Marcus, and Dan and Mary took advantage of the hot mineral baths that they claimed rivaled the best in Europe. There were two tubs, housed in separate small cabanas, with the water from the hot springs piped in.

Francis went to the gym to work out under Peter's capable instruction.

When Nora announced that she had brought with her a couple of brand new decks of playing cards, an impromptu bridge game was organized with Molly, Abigail, Marian, and Nora as the players. Upon request, the staff set up the card table and chairs while Nora went off upstairs to get her playing cards. The late afternoon passed pleasantly; they played until nearly dinner, the intensity of the game holding their attention.

When the dinner hour arrived, and everyone went in to be seated, again Harvey was not there.

"Where's Harvey?" Marian asked softly, leaning over toward Abigail.

Abigail sighed with disappointment but not surprise. Very quietly so no one else could hear, she murmured, "I suppose that he dreaded having to sit at the table with people he considered beneath him so much that he decided to have supper in his room. I haven't seen him since lunch. To tell the truth, Marian, I've avoided him on purpose; he's been such a bear since we got here. He said he was going back to Spartanburg sometime today to take care of some business; he may have gone and not yet returned—if he had any intention of returning at all."

The conversation was pleasant during the fine meal. Everyone agreed that the weather had been wonderful for

April—warm and so far no showers—how restful yet stimulating the yoga and meditation sessions had been, and how lovely the Manor House décor was. It almost seemed like a politeness contest, Molly thought. The pretense would come down over time, and the interaction would become more natural.

When dinner was over, Erika suggested a walk. Molly, Abigail, and Marian agreed to go; the others declined, Nora claiming a headache. Dan and Mary were tired from a very long and full day. Francis would have gone but decided it was best to let the women have some time together without him. Marcus and Angie wanted to call their children on the telephone; this was the first time they had taken a vacation without them.

Overhead the rising moon was full and shed a glow across the earth, lighting the footpath through the rows of pine trees down to the creek, casting silver glints between the spaces in the boughs overhead. As the four women started off down the path, the air was still warm and had become tranquil. The path was covered with finely crushed stone; fallen twigs and pine needles crackled under their feet as they strolled together.

Molly and Erika deliberately slowed their stride so they fell back a little behind the two sisters. Abby linked her arm through Marian's and they talked softly. From time to time there was light laughter, especially when Marian's children and grandchildren came up in the conversation. Abby was more reserved when talking about her son Tony. She admitted to Marian that Harvey felt that Tony had really made a mess of things, dropping out of college during a recession and unable to find a job. They'd argued about it more than once. She was devoted to Tony, even though he didn't seem to be able to find his way; but Harvey's anger toward him created an enmity between the two. Harvey hadn't seen Tony in a long time.

It was difficult for her to confess it, but deep down Abby knew that their indulgence of Tony, satisfying his every whim when he was a child and even later during his teenaged years, had probably contributed to his irresponsibility. Yet she couldn't refrain from continuing the allowance she still sent to him secretly—without Harvey's knowledge. With resignation she faced the unpleasant truth that Tony would probably never earn his own way but would live on Harvey's wealth throughout his life.

Suddenly they came upon a clearing in the woods with an odd seating arrangement. "Oh, my!" exclaimed Marian. The party stopped, as if on command.

A dozen or more seats were fashioned from tree stumps encircling a campfire site. It had a rather eerie appearance for some reason. "What is this?" Molly asked, looking at Erika, unable to conceal the trace of dismay on her face.

Erika tossed back her head and laughed her tinkling bell laugh, aware that her guests must be afraid that they had stumbled upon some sort of witch-coven activities. Speaking directly to their fears, she said, "No, no, I don't practice witchcraft. Not at all. This is a drumming place. We use drumming as a guide to meditation and relaxation. It helps to free the mind. We'll have a chance for you to try it out later this week."

"Whew, that's a relief," said Marian. "I'm wary of new-age stuff, you know."

"You and a lot of other people. But there's no need for concern. Tree stumps are just tree stumps; drums are just drums. There's no magic involved. Am I making any sense?"

Molly smiled at Erika's use of her pet phase. Sure it made sense. Any time she said something that was obviously true, she asked a question of her audience that had to be answered in the affirmative. It was a psychological trick she had used for years to persuade others to accept her point of view. Get them to agree on one point, and agreement on other points comes easier—a sort of mental momentum. More often than not, it worked.

"Let's sit for a while," Erika suggested.

So they did.

Erika spoke with gentleness of the sights and sounds and smells surrounding them. It was peaceful and pleasant. They even tried to drum and laughed at their awkward attempts. By the time they rose to return to the Manor House, all four women were in a positive and relaxed mood. As they approached the rear veranda, all they could hear was the melodious tinkling of the wind chimes barely swaying in the near-still air.

Good nights were said as the four women headed off in different directions, all but Abigail to their respective rooms.

The minute Molly got into her room, she kicked off her shoes as she felt for hairpins holding her hair up, letting the sandy curls cascade down her shoulders. Then she lay down on her bed; it was still early, not yet ten o'clock. What a day, she mused. What a wonderful day. She couldn't remember when she had enjoyed a day so much. Relaxed and content, she felt herself begin to doze off.

Just then, it seemed, a woman screamed and screamed and screamed. Still half asleep, Molly thought she was back home in Columbia. Absurd, inappropriate thoughts flitted through her mind: What was the screaming about? One hardly knew what to think . . . screaming from fear or assault was one thing, but nowadays modern young women seemed to scream out of nothing more than bad manners. Did one check for the cause of the screaming or did one wait until the rude outburst was over? She had observed a young woman in the neighborhood park just the other day, screaming her heart out. Yet no one was near her or bothering her at all. The screaming finally ended in an outburst of obscenities. No manners at all. Was it due to television and movies or bad parenting or something else?

Then she awoke fully and realized where she was. Jumping up from the bed, still in her stocking feet, she ran out of the door, forgetting her slippers. The screaming was coming from the Rugers' room; already most of the other guests were rushing toward the door of Room 7.

It was Abigail screaming. When she returned from the walk with the other women, instead of going straight to her room, she had stopped downstairs for a cup of chamomile and hibiscus tea to help her sleep—and to make sure Harvey had plenty of time to be sound asleep before she reached the room. She had sat downstairs in the parlor by the window in the rocking chair with carved, wooden goose heads for arms and watched the moon starting to slip toward the west as she sipped the comforting tea. When she felt that it was late enough to be sure Harvey was asleep, she rose from her chair.

The house was quiet; everyone had gone to their rooms for the night. Abigail walked softly to her room, started to use her key to unlock the door, and saw the door was not only unlocked but also slightly ajar. A slight pressure from her hand on the door was all that it took to swing it open far enough for her to see inside. Immediately she noticed that the bed, placed directly in front of her facing the door, was empty. Her eyes swept the room automatically in response to this unexpected finding. Something was heaped on the floor by the closet door. "Harvey?" she said as she flipped on the light. And, yes, it was Harvey. She dashed over to where he lay; she knew immediately that he was dead. Then she screamed.

13

Someone Call the Police

When Molly arrived at Room 7, Marian had her arms wrapped around Abigail, trying in a low voice to persuade her to leave the room. Abigail was jerking about, trying to get free and return to Harvey's side, sobbing but without tears. Most of the guests had bunched up in the hall outside the room; some were drifting inside, shocked at the scene, creating a muddled commotion. There were gasps and confused shouts. Right away Molly could see that there was blood on Harvey's head and his body was in an awkward position. It didn't look good. No one could think what to do at first; then Marcus said, "Maybe we should call the police," and reached for the telephone on the table just inside the door of the Ruger room.

"Wait, Marcus," Molly's conditioned response prompted the interruption. "Let's not use that phone; there might be fingerprints, you know."

Marcus deferred to her judgment, having learned of her law enforcement background during their brief acquaintance.

"My room is next door; I'll call from there," Francis Whitt called out from the hallway. He felt a need to be useful and did not know what else he could do. Not waiting for a reply, he pivoted quickly and slipped away.

71

Marian had led Abigail out of the room, as Erika came running up the stairs to find out what all the excitement was about. Soon she had as much of the story as anyone else there did.

Within fifteen minutes after Francis made the phone call, the first uniformed officers arrived. They secured the crime scene and called the Chief Detective and the Coroner. While they waited, except for Abby and Marian who were secluded in Marian's room, the guests gathered in the main parlor downstairs; no one felt like being alone.

Erika walked briskly through the room, turning on every lamp to try to dispel the gloomy atmosphere. She even lit the candles in the candelabra that was displayed in the fireplace. "Would anyone like a cup of tea while we wait?" she asked.

There were several "yes's" and a couple of "coffee-for-me-please" responses.

"Molly, would you help me please? My kitchen helpers have all gone for the day."

Molly was a little reluctant to leave the gathering; her instincts preferred that she watch the behavior of the other guests—it was possible that there was foul play afoot and that one of the guests may have been involved. Courtesy overruled intellect: she got up and left the room with Erika.

In the kitchen, waiting for the kettle to boil, they were silent. The electric drip coffee pot was already starting to drip. Erika served perked coffee at meals but kept the drip pot about for quick service at odd hours. The kitchen was located beyond the dining room and down a hallway, so the parlor was not within sight or sound. Erika bustled about with cups and spoons.

Finally Molly said, "Erika, this is so awful. So awful for you too."

"Do you think he just fell? And somehow hurt himself?" Erika was searching for any explanation that could minimize the calamity.

"I'm sorry, Erika, but I don't think so. I looked at his head; it was hit pretty hard. There was nothing nearby that he could have fallen on that could have made an injury such as that. But there is a dumbbell in the side closet door; I didn't have a chance to check it, but I know the police will."

"You're saying then that you think it was . . . foul play." She could not bring herself to utter the word "murder."

"Yes, I'm afraid so. I hope I'm wrong, though, for your sake as well as poor Abigail's." Molly knew only too well how a scandal could hurt a business; she'd seen it over and over again during her professional career.

"What a shock for her to find him that way."

"Did you know the Rugers before?"

"No, not at all. Mrs. Ruger handled the reservations. I had heard of Harvey Ruger, of course; I knew he was a well-to-do corporate executive. Of course, that's not unusual for my guests. I didn't take much note of it. Oh, Molly, what has happened here! What awfulness is at work here!"

"It must have happened while we were out for our walk."

"Or, even earlier. You remember that Harvey did not come to dinner. For that matter, I don't believe I heard Randy mention that he had ordered dinner be sent to his room. Funny, I didn't think of that sooner. For that matter, he skipped most of the afternoon activities." Suddenly she recalled that he had been scheduled for a massage at three o'clock. "The massage! I wonder if he kept that appointment; I'm going to call Barry right away and ask!"

"Perhaps we should let the police ask him?" Molly responded, her voice turning up at the end into a question.

"Of course, you're right. It is late, nearly midnight, and he's probably asleep. No need to disturb him before morning."

The water was boiling furiously, and the kettle was screaming for relief. Erika poured it into the large teapot she had waiting. The cups and saucers had been arranged on a tray as they were talking. Coffee was poured into two of them to satisfy the requests made earlier. Molly set the bowl of sugar cubes next to the cream pitcher. Erika picked up the tray, and together they walked down the hall, through the dining room and back to the parlor.

Detective Bloom had arrived in the interlude, and he was already hard at work. He had a round face with drooping jowls and a receding hairline, accentuating his shiny forehead. The remaining hair was gray, a little wet looking, combed straight back. His whisker stubble indicated that he had not taken the time to shave when he was awakened at nearly midnight. He was a portly man, no longer agile, and his movements were slow. Always direct in his speech, long years of experience had mellowed him, and he had learned that kindness and sympathy would do more than aggressiveness to produce the results he wanted. When he smiled, his face became almost pleasant.

He was standing near the fireplace with Dan and Mary, recording their responses to his questions. The questions were perfunctory; he meant to eliminate as many people as possible, so that he could concentrate on more likely suspects. The coroner was still upstairs with the body, but one glance had convinced him that it was not an accident.

Dan and Mary recounted how they had spent some time in the mineral bath pool and then returned to their room to rest before dinner. After dinner, they were exhausted from the extraordinarily active day and went to their room for some light television. Neither of them had left the room after that. They had gotten sleepy and retired for the night shortly after ten P.M. They had never met Mr. Ruger before arriving at the spa on Sunday and had seen very little of him since. They had heard of him since they did have equity investments and occasionally read the financial pages of the newspaper. Detective Bloom thanked them for their cooperation and flicked his notebook closed.

Erika had set the tray on the coffee table and was pouring tea. Molly was handing coffee to Marcus and Angie. As the Detective turned from his conversation with Dan and Mary, all eyes followed him.

"Would you like a cup of tea, Detective Bloom?" asked Erika. Her voice was pleasant but sounded tired, even weak.

"I'd prefer coffee, if you have it," came the reply. He could smell the coffee aroma in the room.

"Certainly. Molly, would you mind getting a cup of coffee for Detective Bloom?"

"Molly?" Bloom asked. "You wouldn't be Molly May, would you?" He had heard of her and even seen her a few times, but never with her hair down as it was now. With long sandy curls frosted lightly with silver, she made the detective think at first of a certain popular movie star. She had the same oval face with blue eyes, nose slightly tipped under at the end, and full mouth with slightly gapped front teeth that showed when she smiled.

"Yes, I am Molly May, Detective. And you are?"

"Bloom is my name. I'm the chief detective for the county. Nice to meet you, Mrs. May. I've heard about you."

"Thank you. I'm retired now, you know."

"Yes, I'd heard that too. Quite a coincidence to find you here."

Molly smiled in reply and quickly turned to get his coffee.

When she returned and handed him the steaming cup of coffee, he took a sip and looked around the room. "As I'm sure you are aware already, I'll have to ask you all to stay here until the evidence examination is complete, and you all have signed formal witness statements. I'm sure it won't be long. It's fortunate that the accommodations here are so pleasant; it won't be as uncomfortable for you as it could be, will it?" The room was quiet except for china teacups tinkling against china saucers and a low, disgusted snort from the corner of the room where Marcus was standing. The sound was politely ignored.

The Caldwells asked if they could be excused for the night since they had given a statement and were very tired. With the detective's approval, they said good night to everyone and stole away.

"Mrs. Bischoff, I assume?" he said, addressing himself to Erika. "I'd like to speak to you next." The Detective's tone of voice was polite and kind. "Is there somewhere we can talk in private?"

"Yes, certainly. Let's go to my office."

In her office Erika sat at the elegant walnut desk. She was flanked by tall bookcases with glass doors, topped with pots of vigorous philodendron. She invited Bloom to sit in the armchair at her left and began to recount every detail that she could remember of the day, including Mr. Ruger's massage appointment with Barry Kholer at three o'clock.

Detective Bloom took copious notes. His memory wasn't as good as it once was, and one never knew which detail might turn out to be a valuable clue. As the conversation went on, he learned that Erika and Molly were old friends of many years and that Molly was at the spa as an unpaid guest.

Erika wondered aloud how the Detective Bloom had known Molly.

Bloom responded eagerly. "Of course, when Molly May worked in the Police Investigations Division at Columbia, everyone in law enforcement throughout the State heard of her eventually. Several of her cases were included in training programs for young officers. She even taught a few seminars herself from time to time. I'm wondering if she'll be willing to give us her views on this incident."

"No doubt." With that, the interview ended, and they returned to the parlor.

The other guests were questioned in turn. All of the guests, except Harvey Ruger, had participated in the afternoon yoga and meditation sessions. No one reported having seen Harvey after late morning. The guests were all together at lunch, except Harvey, and they all participated in the afternoon events that lasted from lunchtime to about four o'clock.

Between four o'clock and dinner at seven, Marcus and Angie Bella were in a second mineral bath for a while. After that, Marcus went to the weight room to work out, and Angie went to the library and browsed through some decorating magazines. She walked through the parlor and saw the other women playing bridge; she had never learned the game but paused to watch for a few minutes. Then she sat on the porch alone before returning to the room to dress for dinner. Marcus was already there. After dinner, they talked to their children on the telephone.

Nora Pritchard had spent the afternoon with the other women. She went to her room to get the playing cards. It had taken her a while to find them, but she was back downstairs before four-fifteen, she was sure. After dinner, she felt a headache coming on and decided to rest in her room instead of joining the other women for a walk. She dozed off while watching television.

Francis had gone to the gym to work out with Peter's assistance while Marian played bridge in the afternoon. He stayed about an hour and a half, and met Marcus coming in as he was leaving. After dinner, Marian went for a walk with her sister Abigail, Molly, and Erika. Francis thought it best to let the two sisters have some time together without him, so he went back to his guest room, and after watching the news, he spent some time reading a novel he had brought with him.

After questioning each guest and writing down their statements about where they had been and what they had been doing that afternoon and evening, the Detective and the uniformed officers departed, instructing them again not to leave the premises. Bloom noticed that except for Dan and Mary Caldwell, who were together for the entire afternoon and evening, none of the guests had an alibi for the entire afternoon and evening—all of them had a few minutes when they could have slipped away and been alone.

The coroner had removed the body. "Apparent blunt instrument trauma," he was overheard telling the police. "We found a small ten-pound dumbbell on the closet floor; it has stains on it that will be checked, but it looks like it might be what we're looking for. Obviously the time of death was between about four o'clock when he was last seen and about ten-thirty when his body was discovered. We'll be able to narrow the time down some after the full autopsy results come from Newberry." He was assuming that Harvey had completed his massage, and it should have lasted until 4:30 p.m.

Erika voiced sincere apologies to the guests and implored them to ask for anything they might need to help reduce their anxiety. "Would anyone like Valerian drops?" she asked. Nora and Angie agreed to the potion. Abigail had already been given a strong pharmaceutical sedative and was sleeping in Marian's room. Francis was offered the vacant guest room, so that Marian could stay with her sister for the night. The Ruger room had been cordoned off with yellow tape by the police.

They all went off to bed.

Molly lay on her bed, awake and alert. The events of the day whirled in her mind. Finally her investigative genes took over, and she sat up on the side of the bed and reached into the drawer of the night stand to retrieve an object.

Moments later, Molly, miniature flashlight in hand, was on her hands and knees in the Ruger room. It had been thoroughly searched by the Clareton police, she knew, but she had to be sure there was not one more item that had been overlooked. Then she found it; with tweezers she picked up a tiny bit of something, wrapped it in a piece of paper from a pocket note pad and slipped it into the pocket of her robe.

She crawled back under the yellow tape and crept back down the hall to her own room, just around the corner and three doors down. She saw no one.

14

What the Neighbor Saw

Dale Stromb was sitting on his front porch in his rocking chair, notebook in hand, working on next Sunday's sermon in a joyless, perfunctory way. Keeping the church attendance up had been a challenge, to say the least, and he admitted failure if only to himself. Offering-plate receipts were down and with it his own small income; debt collectors had been calling him for a while now. Preoccupation with his financial woes disturbed his focus on the task at hand; he looked up to watch the cars as they passed by on the way to the spa.

He lived on the live-oak lined lane between the main road and the Clareton Manor Wellness Spa. From his advantageous elevation, he had an excellent view. He tried to catch a glimpse of the occupants to see what sort of people they might be and to distract himself from his problems. Living alone for nearly half a century in a small Southern town can hone one's curiosity about folks from the world outside. Dale had a natural interest in people anyway, a fact that more than likely formed at least part of the basis for his call to the ministry.

It was Tuesday afternoon, a warm, sunny, lazy late spring day. As he looked up, he noticed the little blue Japanese car turn down the road toward the spa, blond hair flowing out the passenger-side window. Latecomers? he thought to himself.

He'd seen a half dozen or so cars pass the day before, mostly late model expensive cars, but there had been one taxi too, on Sunday night.

Dale Stromb, the pastor of one of the small local churches, was often seen about town during the week, occasionally with curiously bloodshot eyes. He was given to what is known in political circles nowadays as "spinning," a term used to describe a form of double-speak that shades a lie so that it sounds like the truth. It evolved from a desire to please everyone all the time, a goal that President Abe Lincoln claimed to have found elusive. Poor Dale seemed to feel some sort of duty to view things as they ought to be, not as they are.

With church attendance down to a record low level, Dale often found himself with a good deal of spare time on his hands. As a result, he had taken to visiting shops downtown and talking to anyone who would listen. To tell the truth, idleness had even led him into the sin of nosiness; he was fond of discussing the troubles of various townspeople, under the guise of pastoral concern.

Pastor Stromb lived in the modest house on the hill that was the only other dwelling on the lane to the estate where Erika's spa was located; it was nearly a mile down the shady lane off the main road to the village of Clareton. There were Strombs and Hardwicks in various combinations in Clareton by the bushels, and they were all probably related to each other somehow, if only centuries back. Many of them, like the Reverend, had never really moved away, except for college-dorm tours, and they and their families were well known in the village. Dale had attained middle age without acquiring a wife, which led some villagers to raise eyebrows and whisper, and others to arrange dinner parties to which he and various eligible young women were invited, to no avail.

He turned back to his notebook and struggled to come up with a few inspiring words. If none came by the weekend, he'd revert to Plan B, which he had used in the past—there were lots of preachers nowadays who posted their sermons on the World Wide Web. He never copied exactly, but he picked up a few good ideas now and then. The Clareton town folk tended to lag behind society at large in the acceptance of new technology; few of them owned computers, and there was none in the public library, either. And he knew for sure they preferred sex and violence on television to religious programming. So far he had caught no whiff that anyone was on to his methods.

To his surprise, less than half an hour later, he spotted the same blue car, going in the opposite direction, much faster this time. The driver was a young man with dark hair. How odd, he thought. But he brushed it off as perhaps a delivery of some sort, some vegetables or flowers. But it was odd, even for a small, country town, for deliveries to be made by an attractive young couple in a small sedan. Oh, never mind, he thought to himself, as he turned his attention back to his notebook and pen in his hand.

That night about midnight he didn't hear or see the police cars as they passed by on their way to the spa; there were no sirens, but he couldn't ignore the traffic the next morning on the usually quiet lane. He noticed Ernie Snale over on the manor grounds near the boundary of his property and hailed him to come over.

"Ernie!" he called. "Come on over a minute, can you?"

The Reverend's house was one of Ernie's favorite hiding places when he wanted to relax a while without being seen by the spa staff, especially Erika. Ernie and Dale were kindred spirits; neither was fond of labor and both could talk endless hours about the most mundane matters. Once they had a twenty minute conversation about how wrong it was for the Town of Clareton to renumber the houses on the town's streets without reimbursing the homeowners for the cost of replacing the number signs on their houses. Trivial nonsense would do as a conversation topic when scandals were scarce.

Casting a quick glance over his shoulder to make sure no one was around, Ernie sneaked over to the pastor's front porch as directly as he could go.

As soon as Ernie got close enough that Dale could speak to him without shouting, he asked, "What's going on at Erika's place?"

"Let's go inside," Ernie responded, looking over his shoulder once again.

As the screened door slammed behind them, Dale asked, "Can I fix you some of my special 'ice tea'?" It was only nine o'clock in the morning, but Dale thought Ernie looked pale and might need refreshment.

"Ya know, Reverend, I generally don' touch the stuff before lunchtime, but today is diff'rent. I could use a glass of yore 'ice tea' fer shore today." Ernie was clearly shaken.

Dale went to the kitchen to prepare the drink, reaching for the vodka and rum setting on the counter. He did not press Ernie; he knew he would tell him what was going on as soon as he got his wits about him. The tea would help.

After a few gulps, Ernie began his story. "I came in to work this mornin', 'bout eight, as usual—maybe a few minutes later. They was po-lice cars all over the place. I made straight for the kitchen; Randy an' Chantal was there, fixin' breakfast. Faye was there too—she's one of the day maids, ya know; Doris, the other'un wont there yet. 'Wha's up?' I says. They both looked scairt outa their wits. Well, it's somethin' awful, they says, one of the guests has been bashed on the head! An' he's dead! They carried him out las' night, Miz Bischoff says. Well, I asked who done it, but they said the po-lice don' know—thought it might be one of the others—one of the other guests, you know—questionin' all of them—won't let them leave. Miz Bischoff, she tole Faye to go clean up the dead man's room as soon as the po-lice was through in there; and Faye said she was too scairt and wanted to wait 'til Doris came. Wanted Doris to go wit her. Don' blame her for that, do you?"

"No, I sure don't. Wow! I can't believe this!" Dale sounded incredulous.

"Well, believe it, 'cause it's true, shore is."

Dale was leaning forward, lapping up the story. Not much happened around these parts; not much that was this exciting. Deep in his subconscious, a light blue Japanese car drove through the back of his head.

"Who do you think it was, Ernie? Could someone have sneaked into the house after everyone was in bed? How hard is it to get into the house —I mean, for an uninvited guest."

"I don' know, man! I wont even here when it happened! I left early yestiday afternoon. This is one time I'll admit it. I left about three o'clock. They was all still in the chantin' room when I left. Miz Bischoff, she never even seen me go." Ernie was still shaking somewhat with fright, but the 'tea' was calming him.

"What's going on over there this morning?"

"I din't look, but Randy an' Chantal tole me that the police detective has got 'em all in the main parlor room, askin' them where they was yestiday evenin' and if they know'd the dead man."

"Who was it? The dead man, I mean?" Dale was trying to get all the information he could, and Ernie's story-telling pace was too slow for him. "More tea, Ernie?" Maybe that would help.

"Sure, jus' a l'il more," Ernie replied, handing over his empty glass. By this time they were both in the kitchen. Ernie was sitting on the edge of one of the kitchen chairs.

As Dale freshened up his glass, Ernie continued, "It was some rich guy from Greenville or Spartanburg, or somewher's up in there. President of some comp'ny or somethin'. Name was Luger or Roger, I forgit exac'ly. Not in the paper this mornin' yet, is it?"

"I didn't see it. I guess the reporter over at the *Daily Standard* will be reading the police reports later on today and pick it up. As soon as he gets up—ha, ha!" said Dale. Aside from town council meetings and a daily trek to the police department to see if anything happened overnight, there wasn't much reporting going on. The newspaper was made up mostly of advertisements and AP copy.

Ernie went on an on about what he knew about each of the guests, what they wore, what they looked like, who most likely had some scandal in the past, and any other vulgar gossip that he could dream up. After his third glass of 'tea,' he felt a little wobbly. Standing up, he said, "Well, I guess I'd better be goin'. It's almos' lunch time. Who knows, the cops may want to talk to me too."

Reverend Stromb was too excited to write any more on his Sunday sermon. He stood on the front porch, left arm wrapped around the porch column to the left of the stairs, and waved to Ernie as he watched him sneak off back toward the spa. "Let me know what you find out!" he called after him.

Part III

Molly's Muddle

15

Back in New Orleans

Cindy was sitting in the well-worn sling-back chair, trying to think of nothing at all. Her head leaned back against the chair, her eyes closed. Trying to calm herself, she took deep, slow breaths, but they had little effect on her restive mood.

On the way back to New Orleans, Tony had not said much; exhausted from the ordeal, Cindy slept most of the way. Back in their dilapidated efficiency apartment, both of them got a little sleep, and then Tony went out.

Cindy was alone, trying to chase away the thoughts that bombarded her mind. What had she gotten herself into? She was sure Tony had stolen something, but what it was, she did not know. If he got caught, she would be right in the middle and from the true crime stories she had watched on television, she knew that the police would believe she knew more than she did about what happened. She was an accomplice—to what? Images of herself in an interrogation room, viewed from above, being hammered by questions from trench-coated antagonists forced open the window into her brain and kept climbing in, one after the other.

She heard herself release a heavy sigh. "Cindy," she told herself, "you have watched enough television news and read enough newspapers to know that only a small percentage of

87

criminals are ever caught. Tony won't be caught." But as she said it, ambivalence surged within her. She didn't like crime or criminals—she wanted them all caught and given stiff penalties—jail time. But she didn't want to be caught up in it herself; she didn't want to be falsely accused. And she couldn't bring herself to want to see Tony caught and in jail. "Now you see it from another perspective . . ." she said out loud.

The jarring ring of the telephone crashed into her thoughts. She grabbed for it before it could ring a second time—when she could afford it, she would get one with a gentler sound. "Hello?" she said.

"Hello, may I speak to Tony, please," a woman's voice said in the earpiece.

"He's not here right now. May I ask him to call you?"

"Where is he? Do you know when he will be back?"

"May I ask who's calling?" Cindy responded politely. She felt the hair on the back of her neck standing up as any remaining vestige of calmness seemed to seep out of her pores.

"This is his Aunt Marian. Marian Whitt. I have some bad news. Very bad news, I'm afraid."

Cindy's heart paused and then began to beat faster. "Well, he said he was going pavement pounding to try to find some kind of job. Our money's getting kind of low. He's been gone a couple of hours; he should be back any time now." That is what Tony had told her, but she knew it wasn't true. He was gone on business related to the safe-deposit box contents, but what that might be, she had no idea.

"Are you Cindy?" asked Mrs. Whitt. Abigail had told her about Tony's new friend.

"Yes, I am," she admitted hesitantly, wondering what her caller might know about her.

"'His mother mentioned you last evening when we were talking. She said you seem to be a very kind person. She thinks Tony may be in love. I hope so. When he hears the news I have to tell him, he'll need to be with someone."

"Can you tell me? What has happened?" Cindy hoped Mrs. Whitt would decline to divulge to her whatever awful news she had.

There was a short pause, and then Marian answered. "Yes, I'll tell you. An awful tragedy has occurred—his father is dead." Her voice was quivering. "We are at the Clareton Manor Wellness Spa. That is, his parents and Uncle Francis and I. He—his father—was—I don't know how else to tell you, except to say it directly—the police believe he was murdered."

Cindy gasped and sat down on the nearest available perch. Oh, no, she thought. No! Surely Tony didn't . . . couldn't . . . Her consciousness seemed to be swirling down and down into a vortex.

"It happened yesterday—afternoon or evening—they're really not sure yet. Tony's mother and I were out for a walk—it was such a beautiful evening, so calm and peaceful. When dear Abby opened the door to her room after we returned, she saw Harvey on the floor. His head had been bashed in!" She blurted it out and then choked back a sob. "The spa has a local doctor on call; he came out and gave Abby a sedative that made her sleep all night. She's awake this morning but hasn't been out of bed. She asked me to call Tony."

Cindy was so terrified she could hardly speak. She knew she must take charge of herself and say the right things. Her first impulse was to demand that Marian pin down the time of the incident, but she reminded herself that she had already been told they were not sure. "Oh, Mrs. Whitt! I can hardly believe this! Tony will be devastated!"

"I know, dear, but he must be told as soon as possible."

"Of course. Where are you now? Where can he reach you?"

"We're all still at the spa. The police have asked us all to stay until they have finished the preliminary investigation at least. It seems that we've all become 'persons-of-interest,' as they say, at the moment. If Tony could come to his mother here, it would be a great comfort to her."

"Oh, yes, certainly, Mrs. Whitt. Shall I tell him, or shall I ask him to call you when he comes in?"

"Please break the news to him, if you will, my dear. It would be better if he heard it from someone in person rather than on the phone. I called last night, but I didn't get an answer. I suppose you and Tony were out. Tell him to come as soon as he can."

Avoiding the implied question about where they were the night before, Cindy felt obligated to promise that they would be there no later than the following day. At this point, Cindy was sure Tony would agree. She made the promise. Then after giving Cindy the number at the spa where she could be reached, Marian hung up the phone.

It was past lunchtime when Tony walked in the door. "Cindy," he called out, "I'm back. What's for lunch?"

Cindy came out of the little kitchen nook and stood just inside the doorway looking at him, trying to recall the exact words she had practiced saying to him when he returned.

Noticing the look of shock and dismay on her face, he rushed up to her, grabbing her arms. "What's the matter?" he was almost shouting. "Are you hurt? What's wrong?"

She pulled back from him and said, "Tony, sit down. Something has happened. Sit here." She pointed to a chair; the springs squeaked when he sat down. She knelt by it, placing her hands on his arm, avoiding his eyes.

Tony's heart sank within his chest; it sank down and down until he felt it in the pit of his stomach. It must be the police, he thought. He had been discovered, and the police had been here looking for him. Luckily he had been out—he could still get away.

"Tony, I have some bad news. Your Aunt Marian called this morning. She said your father has . . . I don't know how else to tell you, Tony; he's dead."

Tony leaped up from the chair as if he had been struck by a thunderbolt. "No! No! It can't be! He was fine yesterday; I saw him!"

"What do you mean, you saw him! You said that he didn't see you, that no one saw you, except an old woman!"

"I didn't want to tell you, Cindy, because I know how you worry about things. But at the spa, after I got inside the room to look for the key, I heard someone at the door, so I hid in the closet. Dad came in. He got something from the dresser—cigarettes, I think—and went into the bathroom. He didn't see me. I already had the key, so I got out of the room as fast as I could. But he was fine! I saw him!"

Tony's wits slowly returned to him enough for him to ask what had happened. "What was it? A heart attack? A stroke?" Thoughts raced through Tony's mind. A man of Harvey's habits could not be in good health at his age. Perhaps the stress had finally gotten to him. Ironic—when he went to a wellness spa for a rest, there he succumbed to his lifetime of bad habits.

Before Cindy could answer, he added, "It must have been a heart attack. I knew those cigarettes would get to him eventually."

Cindy was holding his hand and trying to look into his eyes, trying to search for the truth inside him. "I'm so sorry, Tony, but the police believe he was murdered. Your mother found him last night when she went up to their room. He was lying on the floor; his head had been bashed. Your mother wants you to come as soon as possible." Not wanting to believe that Tony could commit such a heinous crime, she refused to let herself consider the possibility. Still, they had been there, after all, at the scene of the crime. She felt numb.

Tony felt like swooning, but he steadied himself and sat back down in the chair. The springs squeaked again. "We'd better fly," he said. "Mother will pay for the tickets, I'm sure." He was thinking that he did not want to take the blue Toyota sedan back to Clareton, for fear that someone had seen it and would recognize it. Also, he hadn't been able to cash in the loot from the safe deposit box, and he did not want to get picked up with the goods.

Then he caught himself thinking that money would no longer be a problem for him; he could undo his crime and return the gold coins. Everything his father had would belong to his mother and him now. He pushed the thought from his mind. I'm exhibiting my father's character, he thought, thinking about financial gain at a time like this. He was ashamed of himself.

Tony heard himself saying, "My father and I did not get along; everyone knows that. I don't deny that. Our values were at opposite poles. But that doesn't mean I wanted to see him dead—much less murdered—and I certainly did not do it! You know that, don't you, Cindy? My father was fine when I left the room! You do believe me?"

"I believe you, Tony," Cindy replied gently. But did she?

"Start packing, Cindy. I'll call Aunt Marian and the airline."

Her hands slid reluctantly from his arm, and she slowly rose and turned toward the bedroom, watching him. She had just unpacked from their last trip to Clareton. They had been home only a matter of hours; but she was not one to put things off, and she liked things neat and in their place. She pulled the suitcases out again, placed them on the bed and opened them. As she packed, she lectured herself on the necessity to not let anything slip out of her mouth when they arrived at Clareton about a previous trip there. No one must know. She had to protect Tony if she could.

A few hours later, they were in the air, on their way to Columbia, where they would pick up their reserved rental car and drive to Clareton.

16

A Sad Wednesday at Clareton Manor

After having been up most of the night, Erika rose much later than usual on Wednesday morning. All of the guests had been up late too, and she did not think they would expect breakfast on schedule, considering the circumstances.

She dressed and went to the kitchen where she found Randy Yazid, the cook, already there, wondering why she was late. He had left the Manor House right after the evening meal service on Tuesday and gone to his cottage, which was a quarter mile down a hill and around a wooded curve; he had not heard the screaming and had even slept through the police visit. There had been no sirens.

"Oh, there you are, Mrs. Bischoff! I've been waiting for you—I didn't know if there had been a change in the breakfast schedule. I didn't see anyone around. I've made the coffee and started the potatoes." His tone was quizzical.

"Something has happened, Randy. Sit down a minute and I'll tell you all that I know about it." Her drained voice expressed her feelings.

She gave him a synopsis of what had happened the night before. Randy's dark eyes seemed to stare in disbelief, but he held his emotions in check. He mumbled something appropriate about regretting the tragedy; Erika could not discern what he was thinking.

"Since we were all up well past midnight, let's plan to have breakfast at half past nine. I wonder if anyone will have an appetite."

"Yes, madam," was all that Randy said.

Chantal and Faye, the day housemaid, had arrived and had gone outside to sit on the stoop when they found that the day's events were on hold. After Erika left the kitchen, Randy called them back inside.

"What's goin' on, Randy?" Chantal asked. "We saw a police car coming down the hill to the front of the house."

Randy avoided her eyes when he responded simply, "One of the guests was murdered last night."

Chantal shrank back a little and Faye clasped both hands over her mouth to stifle a shriek. "What? Which one?"

"Who?"

"Tell us what happened!" Both were speaking at once.

"I'm not sure," Randy replied. They only came the day before yesterday, you know, and I haven't learned their names yet. I think it was one of the older gentlemen, the wealthy one—Mr. Ruger, is it? The one who had lunch sent up yesterday—and didn't have dinner here at all. Funny, I assumed he must have gone out to a restaurant, but, you know, he might have already been dead. Last night I was feeling insulted and sorry for myself because he didn't want to eat my expert cuisine—but maybe he wasn't able to. I should have checked on him myself!"

Chantal sat down in a kitchen chair next to Faye, who had already acquiesced to her failing knees. Her deep eyes were wide and shining. "What does Mrs. Bischoff want us to do?"

"We'll have breakfast as usual, with the usual menu, just a little later than normal. We'll serve at half past nine. You can finish peeling the potatoes for the home fries; I've already started them. We'll have plenty of time this morning for everything."

"Nine-thirty. We could kill a hog and make bacon by that time. Ha!" As soon as she said it, Chantal recognized the bad taste. "Sorry," she added. "No time for jokes, I know."

"But at least he was a rich guy and not one of us."

Randy turned and looked at Faye, who had just spoken. There was no verbal reprimand. "She'll be expecting you to clean the rooms a little later today. That includes Mr. Ruger's room once the police are finished with it. You might want to start in the common areas if you want to get off work on time."

"What I want today is to get off early! I want to get out of here. I don't like this. I wonder where that Doris is—always late, leaving me to start things." Muttering to herself, she went to the closet to retrieve her cleaning supplies.

When Ernie, the gardener, arrived at the kitchen door, Faye went back to the kitchen to listen again as Randy repeated the story as briefly as possible for his benefit.

"I ain't cleanin' the murder room until Doris gets here, that's for sure," Faye complained. "I ain't ever done nothin' like that before. The laundry will wait for Doris; I'll not touch the bedding in that room. What kind of place is this anyway? I'll have to see about findin' me another job." Faye had worked as a licensed practical nurse on the night shift at the nursing home in town, but due to her brusque manner with the often equally curt elderly patients, that had not worked out well. She was a new hire at the spa; Erika hoped that as a day maid, she would have limited contact with the guests. Her work was excellent. Contrasting with her shaggy bottle-auburn hair, her roots were gray and her eyebrows were dull black. Three of her front teeth were missing in her lower right jaw, giving her mouth a sideways twist when she spoke and her sallow skin testified to years of a night-shift work schedule. Thick eyeglasses completed the plain look, which contrasted sharply with Chantal's glowing beauty.

As soon as he got all the details he could pry out of Randy and Chantal, Ernie shot back out the door.

A pall settled over the kitchen as breakfast preparations were completed; Randy and Chantal did not speak to each other except when necessary to do the job at hand.

By nine-thirty the guests had been called to the dining room. Erika moved Molly's place at the table to her right, where Harvey had sat the day before, not wanting to dramatize the awful event by leaving the chair empty. Most people would flinch when asked to occupy a chair or house or car or whatever of a recently murdered person, but Erika knew that Molly was sensible and would understand the need.

Abigail's place was still set at the foot of the table, but Erika did not expect her to leave her room. She gave Randy instructions to serve Mrs. Ruger's breakfast in the Whitt's room, where she was staying.

Breakfast was a sober affair. Dan and Mary made polite overtures to Angie and Marcus. Nora said hardly a word to anyone. The food was passed in silence. Molly noted that Francis seemed to be the only one whose appetite was not hurt by this dreadful business.

He heaped steaming, aromatic home fries onto his plate, gently pushing the mound of scrambled eggs closer to a double slice of beef tenderloin. There were three biscuits, butter oozing out the sides, on his bread plate. Focused as he was on arranging the food on his plate, he did not notice Molly's glance at him out of the corner of her eye.

As Molly nibbled at the scant servings on her own plate, she cast surreptitious glances at the others, taking mental notes of the verbal and nonverbal communication at the table. She was an imaginative, sympathetic, and perceptive person with almost a psychic sense. She was well into middle age before she discovered that she had a knack for understanding the feelings and motives of others. At first, she assumed it was a human quality, generally present in the entire population. Later, she realized that she tended to see things that others did not. Her views were often different than the majority view; but as it turned out, she was usually, if not nearly always, right. She came to understand that she had a gift: Erika saw it in her and called it a gift of "seeing," but it was really a matter of being aware of the people around her, being sensitive to their movements and body positions, as well as their spoken words. And she did not like what she sensed around the breakfast table at Clareton Manor that Wednesday morning.

"More grits, Francis?" she asked, looking past Angie to smile at Mr. Whitt.

"Yes, please," he answered and smiled back. Angie took the bowl from her and handed it to Francis. "These grits are excellent."

Marcus, who had spent some time with Francis in the weight room on Tuesday and had found him to be a congenial sort, spoke up. "Hey, Francis, why is it every time your elbow bends, your mouth flies open? That didn't happen in the gym yesterday."

It was an old joke with gray whiskers, but with the tension in the air, it made everyone laugh anyway. Even Nora smiled.

"Okay, my friend. I'll get you for that. My wife doesn't let me have real butter at home. I have to make the most of my opportunities, you know," replied Francis, laughing.

"Maybe we'll switch to butter when we get back home," Marian added. Then she pushed her plate slightly away from her and asked to be excused. "I'd better go check on Abigail," she explained. Her face showed the fatigue of having sat up most of the night with her sister. She'd had a couple of hours of sleep at the most and needed to rest.

Polite murmurs arose from those seated around the table. "Let us know if she needs anything at all," Erika offered.

Quietly, Angie spoke. "I wonder how long they will keep us here." It was a comment not directed to anyone in particular.

"Not long, I hope." It was Nora, breaking her silence at last.

Molly glanced in her direction, appraising her body language, wondering what was behind her stiff demeanor.

The others agreed in turn that they lacked the inclination to finish out the week—they were all ready to find more amiable surroundings.

Molly's detective instinct assessed the guests one by one. Nora seemed too cold and withdrawn; Francis seemed too chipper for the circumstance; Marcus was sullen, except for his earlier quip; his wife had a tight, worried expression on her face. Erika was as gracious and pleasant as ever, but subdued by the strain; and the Caldwells seemed to be the only ones at the table exhibiting the type of behavior one might expect under the circumstances. They seemed concerned and anxious to help.

However, as Molly had learned the hard way over the years, there is no typical behavior in response to the crime of murder. In most fundamental ways, human beings are all alike; in more complex situations, they are all different. She had seen too many innocent people convicted in the media (and sometimes the courts too) solely based on their behavioral response to an event, but she knew that a person's outward behavior often did not reflect what he or she was feeling inside.

The sound of a voice brought Molly back to the present moment. "It's a dreadfully unpleasant situation for all of us, but nothing any of us might feel can compare to poor Abigail's misfortune and suffering." Mary was responding to the uneasy heaviness in the atmosphere.

By that time, Marcus, looking as if he were about to explode, got up roughly from the table and said sharply, "I just hope I get a full refund. Please excuse me." And he left the room. Angie kept her eyes on her plate.

As Randy walked silently around the table, pouring coffee, Chantal picked up the plates and took them down the narrow hallway to the kitchen. Molly pushed back her chair, asked to be excused and followed her. Catching up with Chantal, she gently laid her hand on her shoulder; Chantal jumped, nearly dropping the plates, and gave a shriek.

"Mrs. May, you almost scared me to death!"

"Oh, I'm so sorry, Chantal," Molly said sympathetically. "I didn't mean to frighten you. I guess we're all a little bit jumpy."

Noticing a beseeching look in Chantal's eyes, Molly asked, "What is it? Is there something bothering you?"

"I'd better not say. That's all. I'd better not say anything. I don't know anything."

"Chantal, you can trust me," Molly replied, curious as to what it was that Chantal "didn't know."

The urge to unburden oneself sometimes overpowers reason and common sense. Chantal found herself speaking, in spite of her determination to keep quiet.

"Mrs. May, they say that you were a cop yourself once. So I guess you can keep things to yourself."

"That's true; I was. And I've kept my share of secrets and then some. I can keep one more."

"It's that Randy," she whispered, looking over Molly's shoulder toward the dining room to make sure he wasn't coming down the long, narrow hallway. "He says he's from Texas, but he's not from Texas! He's from somewhere called 'Delhi'! I heard him talkin' on the phone. 'Give me Delhi,' he said. He's not an American, you can see that for yourself. Maybe he's some sort of terrorist! Maybe he's poisoned the food! Maybe that man who was killed was poisoned!"

Molly smiled at Chantal and said teasingly, "Being a foreigner doesn't make a person a terrorist, Chantal. There must be something else about him that makes you feel the way you do."

"Yes, ma'am, I guess there is. Sometimes I'll be in the kitchen, just workin', preparin' the vegetables, mindin' my own business, and I feel somebody lookin' at me. I turn and look up, and I see him swish his head away! And I know he's been staring at me. He does it all the time! It's spooky, and he's drivin' me mad!"

"You're an awfully attractive young woman, Chantal. I would think you would get that a lot from all sorts of young men."

Chantal grinned and dropped her eyes. "Well, I guess I do. But there's somethin' different, something strange about this 'un."

Molly found the modesty of such a beautiful young woman endearing. She smiled warmly at Chantal. "How long has he worked here?" she asked.

"I reckon it must be about two years now. But he never talks 'bout his family or where's he from, except to say he's from Texas—which he ain't! He just keeps to himself. Finishes the meal and goes to the cottage. Most folks will hang around and talk a little while from time to time, but not him—hush! Here he comes!"

Randy was coming down the long, narrow hallway toward them. With the poor lighting, he did look a little ominous. As he entered the kitchen, Molly smiled at him and told him how wonderful the breakfast had been.

"You're a wonderful cook, Randy. You make the ordinary taste so special!"

"Thank you, madam," Randy replied as he set about putting the kitchen in order. He didn't look at Chantal or speak to her.

With a quick wink to Chantal, Molly said, "I'll see you both later." She returned to the dining room where the guests were rising from their seats.

Detective Bloom was interviewing Marcus in the parlor, notebook and pen in hand. Angie headed that way and hesitated when she saw them, so Molly approached her and suggested they walk out onto the veranda and wait until the interview was over.

The air was fresh and clean, the sky was blue with little white clouds scattered about; the freshly cut green lawn boasted dappled sunlight that sifted through the boughs of the live oaks overhead, providing a disquieting contrast to the gloomy shroud on the mood in the house.

"You know, Molly," said Angie, using her first name, as young people often do with older people today, a practice that

Molly still found disconcerting, "Marcus and I didn't know Mr. Ruger. He barely spoke to us at dinner Monday night."

"Yes, I noticed."

"He didn't impress me as being a very kind person. But I don't want to speak ill of the dead."

"I understand. His behavior suggested a hint of bigotry; I hope that wasn't true."

"I didn't want to say it, but it was rather obvious. Marcus said he'd like to bop him one . . . Oh, I didn't mean to say that. It sounds awful under the circumstances. Of course, Marcus could never consider doing such a thing. Anyway, it's over now, so it doesn't matter what Mr. Ruger thought about me or anyone else for that matter, does it?"

Molly didn't say it, but she thought that it might matter to Marcus—or at least Detective Bloom might think it mattered to Marcus. Instead she made small talk, sharing a few details about herself, hoping that Angie would begin to feel comfortable enough to talk about her own life and Marcus. It worked; Molly soon had at least a sketchy history of the lives of Marcus and Angie Bella, including the details of the event that had landed him in the county jail many years before.

In the parlor, Bloom was questioning Marcus about the entries on the police record he was holding in his hand. Marcus was sitting very still with his jaw clenched and his thumbs folded inside his fists, his replies terse.

Angie returned to the house, and Molly walked down the veranda steps and started toward the arbor. Stopping suddenly when she heard voices somewhere in the foliage off to her right, she listened for just a short while until she recognized the voices were those of Marian and Francis Whitt, having an intense conversation.

"You know what a monster he was to her. In thirty-five years of marriage, he never once gave her any positive feedback.

It was always, 'don't do this, why are you doing that? that's stupid, stop that.' How she stood it, I don't know." Francis was speaking. "Forgive me for sounding harsh, but I can't lose my appetite over the loss of someone like Harvey. He was the proverbial prince for whom other men went poor, not a great loss to anyone, if you ask me."

"I know, dear," Marian replied. "And I'll never forget how, more than once, she came to us bruised and battered in the early years of their marriage. I remember advising her to remove some of those doorknobs if she kept running into them. She couldn't bear to tell us what really happened at the time, although, of course, we knew. And she confirmed it later, after the battering stopped, or so she said." Marian was not unsympathetic to Francis's point of view, but her heart grieved at the loss of the divine breath by anyone, no matter what their shortcomings might have been. "We all have flaws; Harvey was not the only one. Even if we think his flaws were greater than ours, it's not our place to judge."

"Of course, you're right. I get bogged down in the details of life sometimes and lose the big picture."

"I'm sorry to intrude," Molly said, stepping out onto the path. "I didn't mean to eavesdrop, so I thought I'd better make my presence known. I confess I couldn't help hearing a few words. It was Abigail you were referring to I assume."

"That's okay, Molly," Marian said. "It really doesn't matter now. It's just that in a way, as awful as it may be to say, it's almost a relief to have Abigail freed from that marriage. She was never happy. Harvey treated her badly from the beginning. It was as if she were an employee, managing his household, raising his son, and entertaining his guests. Her sense of duty kept her in that marriage, in my view, but duty is a poor substitute for love. Perhaps now she'll receive just compensation for all she's endured."

"Harvey Ruger was a wealthy man, I understand," Molly said, trying to encourage more conversation.

"Oh, yes. He was worth billions, according to the financial papers. Stockholders weren't too happy about that either when most of them lost their shirts a few years ago. Yes, poor Abigail's compensation should be generous, to say the least." Francis's temperament was the opposite of Harvey's. Harvey had sacrificed almost everything to accumulate wealth, which was his idea of success. On the other extreme, Francis had preferred the quiet peacefulness of being at home with his wife and children to the competitiveness of the workplace. His means were very modest, and he hadn't liked accepting this resort vacation from Harvey's coffers, even it if was laundered through Abigail's own account.

"Maybe now she can finally find happiness," he said.

What a way to find it, thought Molly, as she waved to the Whitts and continued down the path to the arbor. She had talked to Chantal, Angie, and the Whitts since breakfast; she tried to play back the conversations in her mind to sift for clues that might merit follow-up. There were suspicions raised, to be sure, but she really could not consider it particularly unusual that Harvey's behavior had sparked enmity in so many people. But was there something to Chantal's uneasiness about Randy? She was beautiful; he was a young man; it was springtime—his looking at her did not seem out of bounds. But why wouldn't he talk to her? Maybe a visit to Randy would be in order, she thought. Maybe Chantal's misgivings could be put to rest. Or not.

17

Ms. Pritchard Doesn't Tell All

"So what's Nora Pritchard got to do with it?" asked Officer Windham. He didn't see why she needed to be interviewed, why she couldn't just leave the premises, as she'd been asking to do.

Detective Bloom, who was in charge of the investigation, had been called immediately when the 911 first responders got to the Manor and discovered they had a possible homicide on their hands. That was last night. The body had been sent to Abbeville for a full autopsy; the results wouldn't be official for at least a week, but Bloom had been tipped off by the coroner that a determination of homicide was expected. The blow on the head was substantial, and, so far, no other possible causes had been found. There were chemical tests that would take several days to complete.

Early Wednesday morning, before breakfast was over at the spa, he and Officer Windham were back at Clareton Manor. Bloom hoped to complete as much of the investigation as possible before the news hit the big city newspapers. The *Clareton Weekly* had not picked the story up yet, but by tomorrow it would be headlines in the *Spartanburg Herald-Journal*.

"Perhaps Nora Pritchard has nothing to do with it," the

Detective replied. "If we can eliminate her as a person-of-interest, then we can send her on her way. Let's be sure we can clear her completely before she leaves so that she won't have to make the trip back here. She's from Atlanta, if I remember correctly what she told us yesterday."

"You're right, Bloom. I wouldn't want to be the one to ask the Executive Vice President of National East Airlines to leave work and come back to Clareton. Nearest airport is in Columbia, and it's at least a forty-five minute drive from there. Best to clear her and let her go, even if detaining her for a while longer runs the risk of annoying her more than we already have."

About then, Ms. Pritchard entered the main parlor where the two men were waiting. There was a stiffness about her gait; her habitual anxiety was not in check on this particular morning: indeed, it may have been more pronounced. She was wearing a conservatively tailored natural-colored linen suit with a pale blue silk blouse that moved in waves as she strode toward them. She was tall and slim but did not wear her age well—the evidence of a stressful career was etched on her face. In contrast her hands were smooth and soft, long fingers with perfectly groomed nails, young-looking hands that had not been exposed to the sun.

"How are you, Ms. Pritchard?" It was Detective Bloom speaking.

"I'm fine, Detective. And you?" Her half-smile was tight and failed to conceal her lack of pleasure in this meeting.

"Fine, thank you."

"I hope this won't take long. I don't feel comfortable with this sort of 'affair'." She couldn't bring herself to utter the word "murder."

"No, I'm sure you don't. It's not the sort of thing a person can handle very well, in spite of seeing it hundreds of times on television.

"We'll try to make this as brief and painless as possible.

You understand that we do have to interview everyone who was here last night?"

"Of course."

"Then let's get right to the matter. Please, sit here." Bloom indicated a chair; he sat in another directly facing her. Windham stood slightly behind him.

"Now, Ms. Pritchard, tell us in as much detail as possible where you were and what you were doing yesterday afternoon and evening."

"Very well. As you know, we all had lunch together in the main dining room at twelve o'clock. That is, except Mr. Ruger. I understand he had lunch sent to his room. After lunch I went to my room and changed into suitable clothes for the two o'clock yoga practice."

"How long was the yoga practice?"

"It was scheduled for one hour, but it ran over—about twenty-two minutes." Lack of punctuality was a great annoyance to her, and after the scheduled quitting time, she counted the minutes. "Then there was a guided mediation session at three-thirty, and I attended that—quite good actually. I felt relaxed and rejuvenated."

"So you went directly from the yoga practice to the meditation session?"

"Yes . . ." She hesitated. "No, no, I didn't. Now I remember. The yoga poses caused my sinuses to drain, so I made a quick dash up to my room for a sinus tablet. It only took a few minutes, and I rejoined the others downstairs."

"Did you pass the Ruger's room on the way to yours?"

"Yes, they're in Number Seven; my room is Number Ten, which is across the hall and down a little way."

"Did you meet anyone? See anyone? See anything unusual?"

"Not that I remember. Maybe one of the staff. I wasn't really paying attention, you know. One doesn't expect to be quizzed later about those things."

"Of course, not. Let's go on then. What happened after

the meditation session?"

"Some of the women and I decided to squeeze in a bridge game before dinner. I had brought cards with me, so I went up to my room again to get them. Again, I didn't see anyone or anything unusual. I may have passed one of the staff in the hall, but I'm not sure. We played cards until almost dinner at seven."

"With whom did you play?"

"Molly May, Abigail Ruger, and Marian Whitt."

"Okay, go on please."

"After playing cards for a while, I went upstairs to change for dinner. At dinner Mr. Ruger's place at the table was empty as it had been at lunch. Mrs. Ruger looked a bit embarrassed, but no one said anything. Then after dinner, some of the women went for a walk, but I came to my room. By that time I had a terrible headache—sinuses, I'm sure—and I just wanted to lie down. I took a second dose of sinus medicine; it made me drowsy, and I must have dozed off, because I don't remember anything else until I was awaked by Abigail's screaming."

"Did you know the Rugers before this week?" Now it was Officer Windham, trying to get the routine questions out of the way so they could let poor Ms. Pritchard be on her way. He was looking down at his note pad, pen in hand, as he spoke, already anticipating checking off another negative answer, but his head darted up suddenly at the tone of her reply.

There was a slight hesitation before Nora answered. Then she answered firmly that she had not. But there was something in her tone that belied her words.

"Thanks for your cooperation, Ms. Pritchard," said Bloom, his professional tone unchanged by his suspicions. "We would appreciate it very much if you could stay one more day—in case you remember anything else, or we need your collaboration on other evidence." He said it calmly, as if there were no urgency to the matter. After her last response, he had a strong hunch that there was something she was holding back, relevant or not, something another day might give her the courage to release.

"Oh, must I? Must I really?" Nora's frustration was spilling over; she tried to maintain proper decorum in spite of it. She was partly successful.

"Just one more day, please, if you don't mind too much. It might be very helpful." Bloom looked at her beseechingly. If pleading did not work, he was fully prepared to use stronger measures.

"Well, all right then, but I'm not accustomed to these matters, you know. It's very trying for me."

"Of course, ma'am. We understand. Thanks so much for your cooperation."

Nora stood up and turned toward the door. The two policemen looked at each other. As soon as the door closed, Officer Windham breathed, "Whew! She knows something. Something she's not telling us—I was wrong about her."

"Apparently she knew Harvey Ruger before now. But why is she reluctant to tell us? Go on back to the office and see what you can find out about her, Windham. I'll stay here and continue with the interviews."

Returning to police headquarters downtown, Officer Windham set about checking into Nora's history, and what he found out was quite a lot. Between "big brother" running unchecked and even amok after 9/11 and the Internet, it wasn't hard to find out most of Nora Pritchard's life story.

Nora's police record showed nothing more interesting than a single speeding ticket two years before. She was Executive Vice President with National East Airlines in Atlanta, which confirmed what they already knew. She lived in Atlanta but was originally from Vermont. She had married once when she was very young, but the marriage had lasted only a few years. There were no children. She had graduated from Vermont

State University with a BS in Economics and then attended the prestigious Rollins Business School in Pennsylvania where she earned her MBA, *Summa Cum Laude.*

Rollins Business School rang a bell. Windham checked some records on the victim also. Not only had Harvey Ruger also graduated from Rollins Business School, they were both students there at the same time. So that's how she knew him, thought Windham. But how well had she known him?

Officer Windham printed out the information he had retrieved from various sources and walked down the hall to Detective Bloom's office to see if he had returned from the Manor yet. Bloom was there. Looking over the reports, his eyebrows went up. "Very interesting," he said, as he dialed the number for Clareton Manor. Soon he had Nora Pritchard on the phone.

Bloom told her what they had learned. She acknowledged she was aware that Harvey had attended Rollins. However, she insisted that she had been truthful when she said she did not know him.

"It is a large school," she said. "I didn't know all my classmates."

"Why didn't you tell us about this when we talked this morning?" the detective asked her. "It would have made it easier on all of us." He wasn't satisfied with her explanation; innocent people usually tell everything they know right away to end the questioning as soon as possible.

"I didn't think it mattered. I didn't know him, and I saw no reason to mention the fact that we had attended the same school decades ago. It's irrelevant. I don't want to seem uncooperative, but I really am growing weary of this entire matter. Can't you just let me go home? My vacation is ruined, and I may as well return to work!" She was clearly vexed.

"I'm sorry, Ms. Pritchard, but your story will have to be validated before we can dismiss you. Material-witness warrants can be obtained as necessary to detain the Manor guests for questioning." Bloom felt that her evasiveness warranted a more direct approach.

"That won't be necessary, Detective. I'll stay at least until tomorrow. I'm too exhausted to leave tonight anyway."

18
A Visit to the Cook's Cottage

Molly went back into the kitchen looking for Randy and was told by one of the serving girls that he had gone to the cottage. Thanking her, she stepped out the back door and headed down the wooded, curved path.

She approached the door of the cottage and was about to knock when she heard an odd, moaning sound, causing her to draw her hand back and peer through the window instead. There was Randy sitting cross-legged, eyes closed, repeating his mantra. She waited for a moment, wondering if she could be forgiven for disturbing his meditation session. Deciding against it, she started to leave when she caught a glimpse of Randy in the window, rising from his position. So she tapped lightly on the door.

The door opened.

"Oh, Mrs. May, hello!" said Randy politely, his face expressionless, as if this sort of intrusion was routine. "Please come in." He stepped back and held the door open wide.

"I hope I'm not interrupting anything?" Molly said.

"No, no, not at all. I've got some studies I must do, but I haven't started yet. So, no, you're not interrupting anything at all. Is there something I can do for you?"

Molly's appraising eyes saw a tall, slender young man with

smooth light brown skin and dark solemn eyes. His face was dominated by a broad smile and was surrounded with straight black hair, trimmed neatly. Erika had praised him profusely, describing his kindness and integrity, as well as his skill as a chef. "It just goes through and through him and comes back out. Am I making sense?" she had said, using the pet expression that always made Molly smile.

Yes, thought Molly, that makes sense. Aloud, she said, "With the unfortunate events we've been dealing with, I felt a need to get away for a few minutes, and since we can't get too far from the Manor House in case the police want to question us, Erika suggested that I might like to take a walk down here to the cottage. She knows how I love old houses, and she felt sure you wouldn't mind showing it to me. She thinks very highly of you, you know."

"And I of her also. Mrs. Bischoff has been very gracious to me, and I've enjoyed working for her and living here in the little cottage. It's small, but homey, and suits my needs. I'd be delighted to show it to you."

So Molly walked around the small cottage with Randy, and they made small talk about the architectural details. Like the Manor House itself, it was over one hundred years old. The kitchen had been redone in recent years and had the most modern appliances and lovely cabinets. Everything was clean and orderly—no clutter, no dust. They peeked out the back door at the early roses that were beginning to bud.

When they finished, Molly finally brought up the subject that neither of them could get out of their minds. "It's so hard to imagine such a cruelty perpetrated at this lovely place. And to think it might have been one of us who committed the awful deed." She paused, waiting for a reply. None came, so she continued.

"I didn't know the Rugers, of course, but they seemed like fine people. Mrs. Ruger sat across from me at the dinner table on Monday night; she couldn't have been more charming. She said she was so delighted to be at the spa that she had wanted to come mostly for Mr. Ruger's sake—he'd been under a great deal of stress of late, she said."

Randy glanced from one wall to the other and back again, as if searching for a posting containing the right words. "How awful for her now," he murmured finally in a noncommittal tone.

"Yes, how awful indeed. At first we thought it was his heart, you know, stress and all. But then . . . well, you know. It turned out to be something else altogether. Poor Chantal is in quite a state."

Molly was watching for a reaction and was not disappointed. Randy started at the mention of Chantal's name.

"What is it, Randy?" she asked. "I really don't want to pry, but there seems to be some sort of tension between the two of you. Why, I believe Chantal is actually afraid of you!"

"I've given her no reason for that, certainly! But I must really get to my studies now, if you will forgive me, Mrs. May." Randy stood up abruptly.

"Yes, of course. Thanks so much for letting me see the cottage." And Molly took her departure, having learned little about Randy. What was going on? she wondered.

Randy Yazid's real name was Ramnik Yazid. Like most natives of the nation of India, after arriving in America, he found that his real name, even though it was simple to pronounce, was frequently corrupted by his co-workers and fellow students, so he adopted an American-sounding name. Not that he liked it; he didn't. But one made sacrifices to get along in a new culture and achieve success. He had many relatives back in Delhi, India, and success would enable him to send money home to his parents. For that he was willing to allow himself to be called by a nickname.

After Mrs. May left, he was alone with his thoughts. He had come to the United States to acquire an engineering degree and secure a well-paying position that would enable him and his family to have a better life than they had known. College was expensive; so he had taken the job as cook to help pay the bills. The job came with living quarters, a real bonus, and the work was intermittent, leaving him time to focus on schoolwork between guest weeks. The meal planning was a little like lesson planning, he thought; once you have it set down on paper, you just repeat it week after week with a little tweaking here and there. Since Chantal and the other staff could do the bulk of the preparation, he had plenty of time for school.

The cottage was small, only four rooms, probably no more than seven or eight hundred square feet, but it was more than he was used to back home and was ample for his needs. The old oak kitchen table with its leaves folded out made an adequate desk, and his textbooks and notebooks were neatly stacked when not in use. He had to use dial-up internet, which he felt was a terrible waste of time, but DSL was not yet available so far out in the country.

Things had worked out well for him for the most part. Maintaining his cultural traditions was the hardest part. With American consumerism swirling about him, he noticed that it took more discipline than it had in India to practice daily meditation. Being at Clareton Manor helped, though; meditation was practiced there by the guests and by Erika, too, he believed, though he'd never actually seen her at it. However, one didn't expect to be observed during a session, of course.

His culture taught him not to overindulge in anything, but he often found himself tempted to eat too much and to even eat meat, since he had to cook it occasionally, although many of the meals served were vegetarian and vegetarian options were always available upon request of a guest. The preparation of food produced his living, but he knew that it could turn into pain when indulged to the extreme—so obvious to him but Americans seemed oblivious to this fact. Even at the spa, where meals were planned with a view toward healthfulness, some of guests would overeat.

And he often thought about Chantal too; she was so beautiful. That was something else he knew he should not do. He avoided talking to her except when necessary in the course of the day's work, and he avoided looking at her even when he spoke to her. He was afraid of letting himself become enamored with her and create negative karma that would haunt him later. He knew that they were too different in culture, temperament, education, and background to ever be able to have a real relationship, no matter how much he admired her beauty and her spunk. He was not even aware his behavior made him appear sinister to Chantal, but Mrs. May had said that Chantal was afraid of him. He would have to find some way to correct that.

Now that this difficult business of murder in his own circle of life had occurred, he was determined to maintain a positive attitude in spite of it all. He felt no need to discuss his personal life with Ms. May, even though she seemed to be a kind and pleasant woman. Besides there were things he didn't want her or anyone else to know. After lunch on Tuesday, he reminded himself, he had returned to the cottage and began a period of meditation before tackling his textbooks. If anyone asked him directly, he would tell them what he was doing on Tuesday. And if no one asked, that would be fine too.

19

The Most Unhappy Marcus

"Do you know what they asked me?" Marcus was about to explode.

Angie was looking at him, her eyes dark with concern. "Shhh," she said, "they may hear you." After Bloom had completed his interrogation of both Marcus and Angie, they had retreated to the privacy of their room.

"Just because I'm African-American. I know it!" Marcus fumed. "I didn't have a thing to do with the murder, but they pick me out because . . . because . . ." He couldn't say it again. His exasperation stifled him. "They asked me where I was between three and six o'clock yesterday. They asked me if I knew the Rugers! They asked me if I liked the Rugers! Well, I sure don't like bigots—you know that!" Marcus was almost shouting again.

Angie kept her tone low, hoping that Marcus would take a hint. "I hope you didn't share your private concerns with the cops, Marcus."

"Sure I did! I'm not ashamed of it."

"But it gives you a motive."

"A motive for what? I don't go around killing everybody whose views I don't share. Besides, if I killed all the bigots in South Carolina, there wouldn't be enough people left to call it

119

a state!"

Angie smiled. Marcus's propensity for exaggeration always amused her. "Poopsie, I just think in this case it might have been better not to tell everything you know. Poor dear Marcus. You just have to express your feelings directly; there's no beating about the bush for you, is there?"

"Don't call me Poopsie. You know I hate that." Marcus relaxed and smiled. "Baby, you know I couldn't do something like this, don't you?" He looked at her pleadingly.

"Sure I do," she reassured him. "But everyone is not as smart as I am, you know. If they were, we wouldn't have the money for this spa vacation," added Angie, thinking of their stock market windfall at the expense of other investors.

"Some vacation! I hope Mrs. Bischoff will refund our money. This sure hasn't been a vacation for me! It's been a nightmare of bigotry and police harassment, not to mention the murder!"

"That fouled the atmosphere for sure. I can't imagine anything more un-spa-like than a murder. Why, Mrs. Bischoff may have to close the place—who would want to come here now?"

"So, I guess that leaves her out as a suspect. She had more to lose than to gain."

"Unless it happened in a fit of rage—she wasn't too happy about his surliness at dinner, I could tell. Maybe she went to his room to confront him. From what I saw of his personality, that would most likely have led to an argument. Things have a way of escalating, you know."

"Angie, you've been reading too many detective novels. Your brain is going to cook."

"You're right. I'm sure we'll get through this ordeal somehow, and everything will turn out all right."

As she spoke, a twinge of doubt shot through her. The fact was she didn't know how it would turn out. She and Marcus had been childhood sweethearts and had gotten married while they were both still in college. They were soulmates, and she felt that she knew him better than anyone else in the world. Everyone who knew him was aware of his temper, but other than a single episode as a teenager, he never lost control of his anger to the point where it resulted in physical violence. He was a barker, not a biter, after all. Wasn't he? But what if a person is pushed too far? Pushed over the edge? Did Marcus have a breaking point that she was not aware of? She didn't know where he was or what he was doing all afternoon. He may have run into Harvey somewhere. Maybe the gym. If only the matter could be settled soon, and they could be on their way back home.

"Let's take a walk and then 'cool off,' so to speak, in the hot springs tub. What do you say, Poopsie?"

"Okay, Dumplin'," he replied sarcastically, giving her a playful punch in the shoulder. "Let's go."

Part IV

Molly Puts Things Together

20

Abigail Mourns with Her Son

The golden glow of the setting sun created warm spots on the carpet, intermingled with shadows. The big canopied bed with its rumpled bed clothes was emptied of its slight burden: Abigail was out of bed, resting in an over-stuffed armchair in one of the shadows. Sipping tea from a steaming cup that she held in both hands, she kept her gaze fixed on one aspect of the stylized floral motif in the carpet. Her face was pale; her hair was awry. She had sent Marian away for more tea; she was alone.

She found herself thinking only about Harvey's positive attributes, not his shortcomings, which were numerous. There were strong visual memories of Harvey with little Tony on his knee, playing silly toddler games, while Tony squealed with delight. Then she saw Harvey at a business cocktail party, surrounded by colleagues and underlings who both seemed delighted with his humor and stature. She saw Harvey's mother, who had passed away a decade or more ago, smiling at her successful son with immense pride. Odd, thought Abby, how the good in a person seemed to linger after death. It was almost as if the divine spirit, freed from the constraints of the body and soul, hovered over family and friends and old familiar places, showing the true spirit of the person . . .

A gentle knock came at the door; it was Marian. "Abby, . . . Tony is here . . ." she said, just her face protruding inside the frame of the door.

Roused from her reverie, Abigail straightened up and leaned forward in her chair. "Tony?" she called out as she craned her neck to see him. He stepped inside the room.

"Hello, Mother. Are you all right?" he asked.

"I'm fine, Tony. I'm so glad you're here." She reached out to him, and he hugged her tightly. And so they remained for a long moment, neither of them speaking.

Finally Tony pulled himself back and sat upon the hassock at her feet. His face was more serious than she had ever seen it; his dimples had disappeared without a trace.

"Tell me what happened, Mother," he begged.

"Where's Cindy? Did Cindy come with you?"

"Yes, she's downstairs. Tell me what happened," he repeated his entreaty.

"I don't know where to begin. I didn't see your father yesterday after lunch time. He had lunch in our room, and then he didn't show up for dinner, either. I assumed he had either had dinner sent up to him or had gone to town somewhere to eat. I was annoyed with him, so I really didn't care. I didn't even attempt to talk to him, to find out why he was not participating in any of the activities. There were lots of them throughout the day, and I didn't miss any. In fact, I dreaded coming up to the room when the day was over, afraid of an unpleasant confrontation. You know your father, how he can be at times. I could tell that Harvey disliked associating with some of the guests; and I expected him to insist on cutting short our vacation and going back home right away.

"After dinner I went for a walk with some of the other women. When we returned, they all went to their rooms; I went to the kitchen and fixed myself a cup of tea and sat in the parlor and sipped it. It had been a wonderful, wonderful day.

I felt happy; I didn't want the day to end with an argument with your father.

"Finally the time came when I could postpone it no longer, and I came upstairs and found the door to our room pushed to but not latched. When I pressed open the door, even without turning on a light, I could see by the moonlight that your father was not in bed. That's when I flicked on the light and saw him lying on the floor. He looked very still and very heavy: he looked lifeless. They said I screamed. Anyway, everyone came running to the room. A doctor was called from town, and he gave me a very strong sedative. I went to sleep and slept until morning. And that's really all I know."

"Are they sure it wasn't a heart attack? Dad was high strung and always under stress, you know. He could have had a heart attack, then fallen and hit his head, couldn't he?"

"The authorities have convinced the police that a fall could not have caused such an extensive injury. An accidental cause has been ruled out, or so I've been told."

"Do they have any idea who did it? Have the police arrested anyone? Do they have a suspect? What, Mother? Tell me!"

"I haven't been downstairs yet today, but Marian told me that the police have been questioning all the guests as well as the staff. No one has been allowed to leave the area; apparently, they think it must have been someone here at the spa. They've found no sign of forced entry, they say. No evidence of robbery either."

"No evidence of an intruder then?"

"No, no one saw anyone other than staff and guests, but most of us were involved in activities most of the day. I still think it's possible that someone could have slipped in unseen."

"Poor Mother. I'll take you home. Would you like that?"

"I don't think I'm allowed to leave yet, Tony. Besides, I don't know if I could bear to be in that big house of ours alone. You and Cindy must stay with me for a while when I do go back."

"Of course, we will, Mother." Tony was concerned and detached at the same time. He felt a cold tingling along his spine. He hoped the pinched-faced old lady would not recognize him. He had never anticipated making a second trip to the spa; he didn't want to have to explain what he had been doing here on Tuesday afternoon. He would have to stay out of sight and not mingle in the common areas.

He went to the door and asked Aunt Marian to bring Cindy up to the room.

When she arrived, Marian left the three of them alone in the room to console each other. Tony and Abigail recounted memories of Harvey in better days, while Cindy sat nearby, not sure how to participate in the mourning. After awhile, Abigail declared that she'd been cooped up in the room long enough and suggested that the three of them take a walk to the garden gazebo.

Tony and Cindy waited outside the room while Abigail dressed. When she came out, Tony suggested they take the back stairs—it would be more convenient, he said, and they could avoid running into the others. They made it out the back door and through the gate without seeing anyone.

21

May, Bloom, and Windham

Returning to the main house from Randy's cottage, Molly opened the back door to the porch and stopped. She heard voices in the kitchen. It was Detective Bloom and Officer Windham. She held her breath and let the door close ever so slowly. She didn't mean to eavesdrop, but her natural curiosity took over the moment: What had they learned? Did they know, or think they knew, who did it?

"It had to be a man," Windham was saying. "It had to have taken more force than a woman can generate."

"Not necessarily." Bloom was speaking now. "Weight training is quite popular with women these days. Haven't you seen the female bodybuilders on TV?" Bloom could use some weight training himself, he realized, looking down at his paunch. Or at least a bit of routine treadmill.

"I haven't seen any bodybuilders around here, not among the women anyway."

"A well-tailored silk blouse can hide the form, you know. Especially with a well-cut jacket over it."

"There you go with that 'Nora Pritchard' theory again. In my view, it's still more likely to be that Marcus Bella. He's a big fellow with more bulk than the best fitting clothes can camouflage. And he has a history of violence. With a temper like his, it's not likely to take much to set him off. And all the guests stated that they noticed how Ruger slighted him and his wife at the dinner table."

"'One arrest for assault doesn't constitute a history of violence."

"Arrest and conviction," Windham corrected. "As they say, there are usually a dozen crimes committed by a perpetrator for every time he's arrested and convicted."

Bloom was poking at his computer notebook screen with a plastic tip. "Now, let's see. What was it exactly that he did say . . ." He poked the tip at the name Bella on the screen, and then on Marcus. Bloom read his notes: ". . . I said I'd bop him for it, for his bigotry, but, of course, I wouldn't. I was just blowing off steam so I wouldn't explode."

"What did you expect him to say, 'So I went and bopped him'?"

"I would expect him to say nothing at all if that's what he did. I think you're on the wrong track, Billy. Some of the others have better motives—like his widow, for example. I wish we knew what Nora is holding back. May not have any bearing on this case, but I can't get it off my mind." On duty the law enforcement officers rarely addressed each other by first names, but negative feedback tended to go down easier when accompanied by gentle familiarity.

Molly's eyebrows shot up—Nora? Holding something back? What was that about? She quietly opened the back door as far as it would go, let it shut with a bang, and clomped noisily into the kitchen.

"Oh, hello, officers. Any progress on the case?"

"Mornin', Ms. May. Very little progress so far. There's not much hard evidence. What's your opinion?"

"Please call me—Molly. I'm not sure I should bring up any suspicions that I might have. Anything I say can and might be used against me in a court of law, as they say," Molly responded coyly.

Detective Bloom chuckled. "Okay, Molly. We wouldn't try any tricks on an old pro, and we're not trying to get you to commit slander. And you're not a suspect. So what do you think?"

"I think that I wouldn't rule anyone out yet."

"What about Mrs. Bischoff. Have you known her long?"

"Over twenty years. She was a young woman, newly arrived from Germany with her soldier-husband when I met her. It didn't take long for him to abandon her with two children. Far from home and with no money to return to Germany, she had to go to work. She had been trained as a massage therapist and had worked at Bad Kreuznach in Germany, so she managed to get herself a job with a chiropractor and earned a little money. In those days, massage therapy was almost unheard of, especially in the south, so she had some very lean years.

"At that time I was working as a guard at the state prison, and being on my feet all day resulted in back pain that sent me to a chiropractor. That's where I met Erika. I saved my pennies to get a massage when I could to ease my pain. Anyway, she was always sympathetic to me and in return, I listened to her problems as well. We became friends.

"I have great admiration and respect for her. Who would ever have believed that a young single mother whose English wasn't all that good could have created a spa like this one through nothing but her own hard work? She's the most tenderhearted, tough cookie I've ever met."

"I guess she'd have to be pretty strong . . ."

"Sure, she's strong," Molly interrupted. "But not capable of murder. Besides she has no motive."

"Weren't you the one who said not to rule anyone out this early?"

"Except Erika. She had everything to lose and nothing to gain by Harvey's murder. The sensation will hurt her business," Molly pointed out.

"Wouldn't a racial conflict hurt her business too?"

"No doubt. But it never got to the point that it was a serious issue."

"As far as we know now."

Molly nodded. "Okay, I'll concede that."

"Maybe she went to talk to Harvey about his behavior and things got out of hand."

"It's not Erika," Molly said. "I'm sure of that. She's not one to let her anger get out of control."

"I agree, Molly, Erika's not the likely culprit. Even if she had a beef with Harvey, so did almost everyone else here. Harvey Ruger wasn't the most popular guy here, but if all the cranky people in the world got knocked off, the population would be a whole lot smaller," Bloom observed.

"Of course, the Ruger marriage wasn't the happiest one, we've been told," interjected Billy Windham. "Mr. Whitt isn't so sure that Mrs. Ruger isn't better off."

"He told you that? Whew! Even if she is, she's such a dainty thing that I doubt she could have done it. Besides, she's devastated," Molly continued, arguing the obvious case.

"Could have had someone do it for her. Hired someone from outside who sneaked in—she could have given him a key. Or maybe Whitt was in on it," Windham said thoughtfully. "He seems awfully solicitous of her. She wouldn't be the first woman to use the age-old alternative to divorce. As for her grief, we learned that she did some acting when she was young, before her marriage. Anyway, it's not uncommon for the perpetrator in a crime of passion to feel deep remorse afterwards." Windham was businesslike and perfunctory.

"I don't know. It seems a little too farfetched to me. Abigail Ruger doesn't strike me as that type. She could have gotten plenty of money from a divorce, and her only child is grown so the child custody complication didn't exist for her."

"Looks like a crime of passion, though, doesn't it? Usually a friend or family member is involved in cases like that."

"Wasn't Barry Kohler the last to see him?" Molly asked, changing the subject. "Did he have anything to say about Harvey's demeanor or mood?"

"We interviewed him," Bloom responded, checking his computer notes. "Let's see now. He said that Mr. Ruger stopped the massage right in the middle of the procedure. Said he had to make an important phone call before four o'clock. Barry suspected he might be having a 'nicotine fit' instead; he could smell tobacco smoke emanating from his pores. Other than that, he said he didn't know anything. He said he took a longer than usual break while waiting for his last appointment of the day. As a matter of fact, his four-thirty appointment ran late—about ten minutes, he said. After completing that, he went home. Stayed home the rest of the day. Watched television."

"He didn't say how he spent his long break between four and four-thirty?" asked Molly.

"No, he didn't, as a matter of fact. We can go back and check that with him." What they didn't know was that even as they spoke, Barry was busy putting his few belongings into a rented storage facility. Within hours he would disappear.

22

A Chat with Nora

The police interview with Francis Whitt had confirmed that he was Barry's four-thirty appointment on Tuesday afternoon. He had lost track of time and arrived for his massage about ten minutes late, he said. Much to Francis's disappointment, Barry did not add the missed time to the end of the massage; he worked until five-thirty and then quit on the dot.

The police staff had interviewed the rest of the staff as well: Randy, Ernie, Chantal, Faye, and Doris, as well as Peter and Christa Bischoff. None of them saw anything unusual. Their alibis were all being checked out. Peter was in the weight room most of the afternoon, and he said several of the guests spent some time there, including Marcus, Francis, and Nora. Guests were asked to sign in when they used the room; in the event that someone was injured, there would be records for insurance purposes. However, little attention was paid to details regarding the time in and time out.

According to Peter, Marcus was in excellent shape. Much to his surprise, so was Nora. She required very little assistance from him; she knew her routine well.

Bloom confided to Molly that there seemed to be something that Nora knew but was reluctant to divulge. He wondered aloud if Molly could gain her trust and find out what was behind it. Molly agreed to try.

She had meant to mention the trivial item she had found on the floor of the Ruger room, but the lure of the intrigue surrounding Nora distracted her. I'll mention it the next time we talk, she assured herself. She didn't intend to withhold evidence, if that's what it was. Most of the time items picked up at crime scenes turned out to be junk, so she didn't want to embarrass herself by making an issue out of nothing—her reputation for nitpicking stung a little.

As she walked down the hall from the kitchen, Molly glanced out a window and happened to see Nora sitting on a garden bench in the arbor. She had a large brimmed white hat on her head and was wearing a fine white sweater patterned with tiny green leaves with khaki slacks that matched the veins in the leaves. Thinking how Nora always seemed to have just stepped out of the proverbial "band box" in contrast to her own hit-or-miss style, Molly casually made her way in that direction.

"Hi, Nora," she called out. "Lovely day, isn't it?"

"Hello, Molly. Yes, it is. Though the sad circumstances cloud the atmosphere somewhat, I'm afraid. It's hard for me to enjoy the beauty and serenity here. Frankly I'd like to go home."

"So would we all. It's just dreadful. I'm sure the police will have the matter settled soon, and we can all be on our way." Molly was deliberately trying to create the impression that she was leaving the entire investigation in the hands of the police, that she was not involved in the least.

Nora gazed off into the forest, watching the breeze sway the tree branches. She took her sunglasses off; her eyes were green, almost a match for the color in her sweater.

"I enjoyed our bridge game yesterday; you're a very good player." Molly was trying to jump start a conversation that seemed to want to stall.

"Not as good as I'd like to be. I don't have the memory capacity for it, even though I do love the game."

"Nonsense, you played brilliantly," Molly smiled warmly. "The strategy is as important as the memory, and you displayed remarkable talent in that aspect."

Nora turned to look at her. "I suppose you're thinking the murderer was also a good strategist?"

"What are your views on it?"

Nora placed her hands on the bench on either side of her and looked down at her lap. "I suppose a lot of people had a reason to dislike Harvey Ruger. He hardly spoke to anyone since we arrived, not even his brother-in-law Francis. Stayed to himself. He must have been a very lonely man. It's hard to imagine that one of us must have done it; everyone here has been so kind and friendly—except Harvey."

Molly's psyche sat upright at the familiar use of Harvey's first name. She continued offhandedly, "According to the police, no one remembers seeing an intruder. Could someone have walked right in and no one noticed with so many people around? There are guests and staff all over the place most of the time."

The mention of an intruder stirred a memory in Nora. "By the way, who is the young, dark-haired man on staff? I saw him early in the week, but I haven't noticed him around today." Nora had a faint recollection of passing a very attractive young man in the hall sometime on Tuesday. Was it in the morning or afternoon? She couldn't remember.

"Do you mean Barry?"

"No, not Barry. He's the massage therapist. Even with my limited memory cells, I wouldn't forget him. And not Randy either, of course. He's of Indian ethnicity, I'm sure. The young man I saw was more European in appearance. Peter, of course, is blond."

"Nora, I think you've just named all the young men who work here. I suppose it could have been some of the part-time yard staff." Molly felt a tingling on the back of her neck. Could there have been an intruder? "We'd better ask Erika and be sure."

"Wait, I'll go with you. Suddenly I'm not sure I want to sit out here by myself." She shuddered as she glanced about. No one was around except for Ernie Snale sneaking back up the road from Reverend Stromb's house. "Oh, here comes Ernie now. Why don't we just ask him?"

"Good idea," Molly agreed, calling out, "Oh, Mr. Snale, can you come over here for a moment?"

"I don't work for them," Ernie muttered under his breath. "Having that ole bitty Bischoff on my case all the time is bad enough. Who in the worl' does that ole lady May think she is? She ain't the cop no more." He was a little tipsy after his visit with Pastor Stromb. He might as well tell them what he thought and get it off his chest.

As he came near, the women caught a whiff of alcohol. "Mr. Snale," Molly began, smiling warmly and tilting her head slightly to one side—a disarming gesture that she'd practiced for years, "Mrs. Pritchard seems to remember seeing one of the gardeners in the Manor House yesterday. Do you know whom that might be?"

"No, ma'am, they wont no gard'ners here on Tuesday. That is, 'ceptin' me, and I sure wont in the big house. No, ma'am. If ya got any more questions, I reckon you better give 'em to Miz Bischoff. Answerin' questions ain't in my job description." And off he went, with a little more bounce in his gait than usual. Women! he thought . . . Always meddlin' in things that wont none of their bin'ness. He, for one, didn't intend to spend his time dawdling around with them. He had work to do.

Meanwhile Nora and Molly just looked at each other quizzically, neither knowing what to say. "I suppose his statement ought to be verified," mused Molly. "Maybe he's just being uncooperative. We'd better check with Erika."

As they approached the house, they saw a teal-colored Grand Am drive up into the driveway. A young, dark-haired man and a young, blond woman got out of the car and started up the front steps. Nora stopped in her tracks. "You know, I think he resembled that young man there," Nora said, nodding discreetly in the direction of the young couple. "Who is he?"

"Let's find out." And they went in search of Erika.

They found her in her office. She was sitting at her writer's desk in the center of the room, flanked by tall bookcases that seemed to be standing guard. Her hands were poised near the keyboard of the computer, but the fingers were not moving; she was gazing out the window to her left.

She had been working on the finances, figuring how much credit she would need to meet the monthly expenses if she had to refund all the proceeds she had collected for the week— and she felt she had no other choice. As heavy hearted over this matter as she was, her practical side kept nudging her with the fact that she would have to put this episode behind her and work harder to get the business back on track. Cancellations for future bookings were already coming in. She couldn't blame people for not wanting to vacation at a murder site; it didn't appeal to her either.

"Erika," Molly said softly, as she tapped on the open door. "May we come in?"

Erika turned to face them. "Sure, come on in, Molly. Hi, Nora. Please sit down." She motioned toward two armless chairs, upholstered in a subtle floral pattern. They sat. "Is there something I can do for you?" She was still a little distracted by the jumble of numbers she had been trying to sort out, so it took a little effort to turn her attention to her guests.

"Erika," Molly began, "Nora thinks she remembers seeing a young man in the guest wing sometime on Tuesday."

"One of the staff?"

"No, we don't think so. He was a good-looking, dark-haired young man. European features and coloring."

"What time was that?"

"I'm not sure," Nora said. "Unfortunately, I was distracted, not paying too much attention. Actually I had forgotten it until this morning."

Molly continued: " . . . so we asked your grounds-keeper Ernie if perhaps a day-gardener had been called in for special work and had entered the house for some reason—maybe taken a wrong turn or something. But Ernie said he had not had anyone here on Tuesday. Is that correct?"

"Yes, that's correct. All the major work was done last week. Ernie comes in every day to keep the place neat—and to goof off, of course. Sometimes I don't know why I keep him on the payroll."

Nora could restrain herself no longer. "Then as we were coming to look for you just now, we saw a young man getting out of a car in front of the manor—he reminded me of the young man I thought I saw on Tuesday. Who is he?"

"Oh, that would be Tony Ruger, Abigail and Harvey's son. He couldn't have been here on Tuesday; he lives in New Orleans. Marian called him this morning and told him what happened and asked him to come here to be with his mother. He was able to catch a flight into Columbia and then drove over—I didn't know he had arrived yet. Was bringing a friend, I think."

"Oh, I see," Nora said. "Well, that makes sense. It could have been one of the staff members I saw, or thought I saw. As I said, I wasn't paying attention. I was thinking about other things. I'm sure it wasn't important anyway."

Thinking about what other things, Molly wondered silently.

23

A Massage and a Message

So far it had been an exhausting day; Molly needed a rest. Soon, Christa was doing a great job of massaging away Molly's stress. Generally, Molly tried to discourage conversation while trying to relax, but under the circumstances, she encouraged Christa to talk. Molly had known Christa since she was a child: Christa called her Aunt Molly.

"The murder of Mr. Ruger has all but ruined this week," Molly ventured, hoping to prod Christa to tell whatever she might know, if anything. "I'm amazed that you can perform your magic as expertly as ever under these circumstances. Now I understand the curative power of the 'laying on of hands,' often mentioned in the Scriptures." She was referring to the deep tissue kneading that was making it difficult to suppress cries of pain.

"Who do you think did it, Aunt Molly?"

"I don't know. I'm hoping you can help me out."

"Me? You know I never divulge anything my clients tell me while they're in my 'torture chamber.' "

"Then someone has told you something?"

"Well, no, not really."

"Come on, you can tell your old Aunt Molly," she wheedled. After all, there has been a murder, and we must get to the bottom of it, mustn't we? So, tell me, Christa dear, which of the guests has had the most knotted muscles this week?"

"I hope knotted muscles do not a murderer make. If they do, I come into close proximity to a bunch of them on a regular basis."

"Who has seemed tense to you?"

"Of the guests? Barry has been the most tense of the persons at the scene, but he's not a guest, of course. He's staff. Of the guests, Francis Whitt has been the most relaxed and Nora Pritchard the most tense. And you did not hear that from me."

"Barry?"

"By now, certainly you've heard that Barry was a stockbroker who lost a small fortune because of Harvey Ruger's corrupt and conniving business practices, or so Barry tells it."

"No, I have not heard that. I'm glad you told me. Do you think he's the sort who might take advantage of an opportunity to get even?"

Christa paused, breathed in a long, slow breath, and resumed her kneading. "I hope not. Barry's a nice guy, and I really like him a lot, but he's human too. There could have been a confrontation and things got out of control, I suppose. I don't want to believe he had anything to do with it. But he has been awfully uptight since he found out Harvey would be here. He did Harvey's massage yesterday afternoon; I guess he was the last one to see Harvey alive. Except the murderer of course."

"I see. Where is he now?"

"He left just a short while ago. Francis and Dan both had massages this morning, and Marcus had the first appointment after lunch, so since he had no more clients today, he took the rest of the afternoon off."

"And what about Nora?" Molly continued.

"I think you should talk to her. She tried to conceal it, but she was crying during her massage. I pretended not to notice, but I'm sure something is bothering her. She's holding something in that wants to get out. I could feel it."

"I'll do that. Thanks for the tip, Christa."

After the massage, Molly felt refreshed. Swallowing at least three small paper cups of water to disperse the lactic acid worked loose in her muscle tissue, she dressed and went looking for Nora. Not finding her in the common areas, she knocked on the door to her room.

"Nora, are you in there? It's Molly," she called out.

Nora opened the door and invited Molly in. It was as though they both knew why she was there. Nora was exhausted with bottling up the sorrow she had lived with so many years, and soon the details were pouring out into Molly's sympathetic ears.

Nora confided that she had known Harvey Ruger when they were students together at Rollins Business School. She had known him very well, in fact. She was separated from her husband, but still married at the time; a much younger, high-spirited Harvey had swept her off her feet. He was intelligent, articulate, attractive, and very attentive to her. The liaison had gone too far, and she had become pregnant. She was thrilled because she had hoped for a baby for years. Through much difficult testing, she and her husband learned that it was unlikely that he would ever be able to father a child. So after learning that her dream was coming true, she was eager to finalize her divorce and marry Harvey and have the perfect marriage and family.

On the day she had learned of her pregnancy, she had prepared a special dinner with candlelight, flowers, and a bottle of expensive wine that she couldn't afford in order to provide the distinctive atmosphere appropriate for delivering such wonderful news to Harvey. However, things did not turn out as she expected. When she made her announcement, Harvey's face turned to stone. He demanded that she do what he called the "right thing" and prevent the "problem" from occurring. And that is what she did; she never had another chance to become a mother.

To avoid the stigma she left school for a while and never saw Harvey again, until this week. The sight of him brought back a flood of tearful memories.

She wasn't sure he recognized her at first. She was much thinner now and had cut her dark hair short and stopped dyeing it blond. Instead of contact lenses, she had gone back to wearing glasses; she thought they made her look more professional for her present career. She had reverted back to her maiden name; Harvey had known her only by her married name. In many ways, she wasn't the same person who was once in love with Harvey Ruger.

Notwithstanding his balding head and expanded waistline, she had recognized Harvey immediately. Her feelings were mixed. This was a man she had loved deeply at one time many years ago, a man who had treated her soul brutally. She decided to avoid him at the spa, but she caught herself a couple of times evaluating and pitying the wife he had chosen.

Nora found herself confiding all this in Molly. She didn't know why except that she had kept it to herself for so many years and the sudden shock of Harvey's death caused the rupture of the dam that had held back her emotions. She began to sob. It didn't matter any more anyway; Harvey was dead. No one could be hurt by the truth. Molly would never tell Abigail or anyone else; she had promised.

Molly was not surprised at the confession; she had stopped being surprised by anything a long time ago. Wondering if she should tell the Chief Detective, she decided not to—unless she found something more to link Nora to the murder. Nora had not admitted to speaking to Harvey at any time on Tuesday; perhaps she hadn't. She felt that she needed to do a little more checking before she passed along any information about Nora's relationship with Harvey.

24
That's Him

Late in the afternoon, after her confession to Molly about her past with Harvey, Nora was sitting in the parlor, watching the shadows lengthen. As she gazed out the window, Nora saw Tony walk to the garden with his mother and Cindy. That's him, she thought; I'm almost certain of it. No doubt there was nothing questionable about his presence here Tuesday. But, if so, why does no one else seem to know about it?" She turned to find Molly entering the room.

She rose and walked halfway to meet her. "Molly," she blurted out, "I am almost sure it was Tony I saw in the hallway Tuesday. And it was afternoon, I remember, because it was when I went to my room to get my playing cards for our bridge game after the group meditation session. As I was returning to the parlor, I met him—Tony—in the upstairs hallway."

This new information threw Molly off balance. Could Harvey have been murdered by his own son? Or, if Tony was able to get inside the Manor House almost without being seen by anyone, could there have been someone else who also got inside?

"Perhaps he came to visit his father for some reason, and no one else knew about it because Harvey did not live to tell about it."

"Of course, that's probably it. If Abigail didn't know her son had been here, he'll tell her now, I'm sure."

"In any case, we'd better mention it to Detective Bloom. He probably already knows about it and has determined that it is not significant, but that's not for us to judge. We must tell him what we know." As she spoke, Molly tried to ignore the nagging voice deep within, trying to remind her that she knew at least two other facts that she had not passed on to the Detective. If and when the right time came, she would divulge them, but for now, she did not see the relevance. And she resented the nudging of her conscience; it was always doing that!

"I'll call him after dinner," she said. "I have his cell phone number and instructions to call him if anything came up." It was nearly dinner time; it wasn't so urgent that she should miss one of Randy's delicious meals for it. She was starving; it had been a long time since her lunch of fresh turkey-on-sourdough with tomato, Vidalia onion, and lettuce leafs picked from the garden within minutes before sliding them between the sandwich slices.

"Let's go into dinner. Let's not tell the others about seeing Tony here yesterday, until after we've had a chance to tell the police. What do you think?"

"Good idea. I don't want to create suspicion where no basis exists. There's too much of that here already."

When they reached the dining room most of the others were already there. Tony and Cindy were seated with Abigail. They were introduced around, and the table conversation was steered away from the recent unpleasantness for Abigail's sake.

After the subdued meal, Molly and Nora excused themselves and went to Molly's room.

"So what did you think of Tony Ruger, Nora?"

"I noticed that he was very attentive to his mother and seemed concerned with her well-being."

"Yes, I thought so too. Nice manners. Seems to be well brought up. Some rich kids can be bratty."

"Can't they though."

"He did seem a little anxious, but I guess that's to be expected under the circumstances. Let's call Bloom."

Molly dialed the number and Detective Bloom's voice came over the line, a little crackly due to the limited cellular technology.

"Detective Bloom, this is Molly May. I may have some new information for you—or you may already know about it."

"Please go ahead; what is it?"

"The Rugers' son Tony arrived this evening from New Orleans. Nora has a strong recollection that she saw him here on Tuesday afternoon."

"What? This is news! Mrs. Ruger nor any of the others mentioned this earlier."

"Do you suppose he came to see his father and avoided everyone else for some reason?"

"If he did, that puts him in an awkward position under the circumstances. Where exactly did Ms. Pritchard see him?"

"In the upstairs hallway, in the guest wing. Actually he was only a few paces from the Rugers' room. Of course, if he came to see his father, that would be the natural place for him to be."

"I'll come on over. This needs to be checked out. I'll be there in about thirty minutes." Bloom felt himself swell with excitement and urgency. From his car, he phoned Windham to meet him at Clareton Manor.

Not wanting to alarm anyone else or to warn the perpetrator, if there was one around, Molly suggested to Nora that they keep the news to themselves until the officers arrived.

They didn't have to wait long. Soon they were standing on the front porch with the two officers, and Nora repeated every detail that she could remember. "You're a good witness, Ms.

Pritchard," Bloom said when she finished. "We'll get to the bottom of this. Windham, you go check with that reverend up the road who's always sitting on his porch when we come by. Maybe he saw something Tuesday and can collaborate this story for us. Meanwhile, I'll talk to Mrs. Ruger and her son."

It was getting cooler outside; Molly shivered in a breeze. Was it just the cold? Something else was bothering her, but she wasn't sure what it was. Nora seemed very eager to tell her story—maybe too eager. Was she trying to defer suspicion to Tony for some reason? Oh, nonsense, thought Molly. It is natural for a witness to want to help the police solve a crime, isn't it? Especially when the witness is impatient to get away from the whole nasty business. There was something else, some other signal, being picked up by Molly's radar, but it was not well defined.

"Molly," Bloom said as he came inside upon his arrival, "I'd like to talk to you later, but right now an interview with the young man in question is my top priority."

The arrangements for a later meeting were made, and without delay, Tony found himself in the library with Detective Bloom. There was the necessary discussion of the tragic events and the extension of appropriate condolences. Then Bloom said, "Tony, let me get straight to the issue. A witness says that you were seen here on Tuesday afternoon. Tell me about that."

"Me? Here? She must be mistaken, officer," Tony replied confidently.

"She? Why do you say 'she'?"

"Well, 'he,' then," Tony replied. "What difference does the pronoun make?"

Detective Bloom went on to recount the details of Nora's description of the person she saw and the time she saw him. Tony stuck to his story. After some time Officer Windham returned from his errand and signaled to Bloom to come outside the room. They exchanged whispers and Bloom went back to Tony.

"Do you own a light blue Toyota?"

"Why, is it parked illegally?"

"Just answer the question."

"I arrived today in a teal Grand Am. It's parked outside. I can show it to you."

"Tony, if you want a lawyer before answering my questions, that's fine. But a resident down the street saw a light blue Toyota pass by his house twice on Tuesday afternoon; the description of the passengers matches you and Cindy. So we have two witnesses who put you here on Tuesday afternoon. You can tell me what you were doing here, or we can go downtown and talk about it. What do you want to do?"

Tony squirmed, realizing it was pointless to continue to deny it. He smiled, dimples flashing. "Detective," he said, "I guess you've got me. I'll tell you the truth. I was short of the cash I needed to pay my rent, and I thought about borrowing it from my mom—she'll never say no to me. But I didn't want to spark a fight between her and dad on their anniversary holiday. So, rather than create a row with my dad—he doesn't approve of my lifestyle—I decided it would be better for everyone if I just 'borrowed' the money without seeing either of them, if you know what I mean."

Bloom noticed that he spoke of his father in the present tense. "I know what you mean; go on," he said.

"I called ahead to make sure they were both out of the room, Dad especially—if I ran into Mom, I could handle that. The receptionist made that easy by telling me over the phone the room number and what Dad's schedule was for the day. So I came in the building; no one questioned me. I had no trouble getting into the room. Took a couple hundred bucks from the dresser drawer. My dad always carries, uh, carried, extra cash with him. Then I left. I passed a woman in the hall as I was leaving. And that's all."

"You and your father didn't get along then?" It was a question, even though it didn't require an answer.

"Detective Bloom, I loved my father, in a way. But we were very different. His life consisted of long hours of drudgery, stress, and confusion. Growing up, I hardly saw him. Sure, we had a big house, a luxurious lifestyle, and everything that we could ask for. But I want more than just "every–THING." I want to live, to hear the birds sing, to smell the roses. I didn't kill him. I'm not a killer. I may not be the best money manager, but I could never do anything like that. You can ask Mom or Cindy! They know me, and they will vouch for my character. For that matter, you can ask anyone who knows me."

"We'll have to check your story, of course. But, for now, let's get your complete statement into the record," Bloom responded, as he flipped open the cover of his laptop computer.

After the statement was entered, Bloom told Tony that he would have to print out a copy at the office for him to sign. He told him not to leave the premises.

As Tony left the room, Officer Windham, who had been waiting outside, came in.

"So how did it go?" he asked.

"Well, Windham, he gave me a statement admitting to being here. He said he came to borrow money from his parents, intending to 'borrow' it without their knowledge. He said he stole a few hundred dollars from his father's dresser drawer. It doesn't make a lot of sense to me. He could have called his mother on the phone, and from the way he described their relationship, she would have wired him the money. It doesn't ring true to me. He lied about being here until we presented him with two witnesses; there's no reason to believe that he didn't just switch one lie for another."

"Think he'll consent to a lie detector test?"

"It won't hurt to ask. We need to run this by the prosecutor and see what he thinks we ought to do next."

"It looks pretty bad. Maybe the old man caught him in the act of stealing the money, and they got into it then."

Molly had approached the library door to meet with Detective Bloom as they had prearranged and had inadvertently heard most of the discussion. I'm making a habit of eavesdropping, she thought.

When Bloom saw her he motioned for her to come in.

"I guess you heard what was said," said Bloom.

"Yes, most of it. Now we've got another person-of-interest to add to the list."

"We've caught this one in a lie, so he goes to the top of the list."

"Actually any one of several people could have done it, though. Abigail is considered to be better off, according to Francis and Marian. She's certain to be wealthy now, without having to contend with a less-than-model husband. Did you notice how Francis' neck turned red when he described how Harvey treated Abigail? He has a soft manner, but there's suppressed anger underneath, if you ask me. I'd bet on it. Maybe Francis confronted Harvey about how unhappy Abby is, and things took a bad turn. And Marian. I don't think she could have done it alone, but she might be in on it. She's very protective of both her sister and her husband, like a mother lion."

"Then there're two others who were angry with Harvey: the young former stockbroker-turned-massage-therapist Barry and even Erika herself. And what about Randy? Who is he anyway? The list keeps getting longer."

"I don't think we can eliminate Marcus Bella, either," Windham offered. "With his history of violence and short temper, I can imagine Harvey provoking him without trying hard."

"Or Nora either. What do you think, Molly?"

"I think I agree with you. I was afraid you were going to eliminate Nora from the list. She seemed so eager to tell you about recognizing Tony that it raised some concern in my mind. I like her a lot, but I can't be sure she's as innocent as she claims to be. There are always two sides to the story."

"What story is that, Molly?"

"Oh, did I say 'story'? It's nothing in particular, just an overused figure of speech that has become a habit with me." Molly was not ready to betray the confidence that Nora had placed in her, especially with Windham present. He seemed too quick to point a finger without first carefully evaluating all the facts. She did not want Nora under the same kind of unfair scrutiny that Marcus had been subjected to. Perhaps she'd tell Bloom in a day or two when no one else was around.

"She seems very nice once you get to know her," Molly added. "One doesn't want to find a murderer hiding under that cover."

"I know what you mean. We'd rather it turned out to be some weasel like that Ernie Snale."

"Maybe we should add him to the list," Windham said with a laugh. Ernie was a weakling and a wimp, and one who drank too much. But no one took him seriously.

25

An April Rain

Molly awoke Thursday morning with a headache and a stiff neck, caused by stress, no doubt. She decided to take an excursion into town to try to relieve the tension and to diffuse the dark cloud that had settled over her mind. There were bicycles available to the guests, and since Molly had left her car in Columbia, she decided to make the trip by two-wheeler.

After taking a quick shower and donning a pair of khaki slacks and a cotton polo shirt, she dashed out, deciding to grab a fast-food breakfast in town. The morning sky was a clear, bright blue; the sunshine comforted the earth. The jubilant life declared by nature on this fine April day was unmarred by the tragedy in the center of the little circle at Clareton Manor.

In no time at all she was in Clareton, latching her bicycle to the rack in front of the post office. She wandered the streets of the indolent village, only half aware of the springtime beauty and aroma that reached out to her from the yards lining the sidewalks. The unique smell of freshly clipped boxwoods, one of her favorites, filled the air. The brilliant pinks, reds, and lavenders of bountiful azaleas created halos of light around themselves. As she walked under the boughs of the dogwood trees, limbs heavy and dropping with white crosses tinged with pink, she began to muse over the evidence that was starting to accumulate.

Poor Abigail was considered better off by almost everyone—and, by herself, as well? Molly wondered. Could she have done the deed? Or perhaps sympathetic Francis had helped her out. Perhaps there was a quarrel, resulting in a threat by Harvey against Abby. Perhaps Francis overheard and came to the rescue. Then the two conspired to keep silent. Maybe there was more to the affection between Francis and Abigail than either Marian or Molly knew.

Then there was Nora.

Harvey had been the catalyst to the destruction of Nora's dearest dream—to be a mother. Then he had scorned her. Her bitter hate toward the man who had jilted her and turned her hope into despair was palpable. In a fit of rage, her strength could be enough to overpower a paunchy, overweight, flabby man like Harvey. The fury that could result from that scenario was the stuff of songs and stories for eons. After the dinner on Tuesday, she had declined to join the others for a walk. Perhaps she had run into Harvey on her way back to the room, perhaps he finally recognized her, perhaps they had a private talk, perhaps her fury boiled over. And she seemed too eager to implicate Tony. But Nora was a refined, cultured woman, not the type one associates with felonies.

And what about Barry, the former stockbroker, Christa's friend?

Barry had been transformed from a prince to a pauper by Harvey's outrageous business schemes. The love of money is truly the root of all evil, and it is as common as jealous love as the motive for crime, she decided. Could Barry have been so vengeful that his grudge against Harvey had not faded? Was it Barry who took revenge? That was hard for Molly to believe; Barry seemed to be a gentle person.

In spite of Officer Windham's suspicions, Molly felt that Marcus Bella was not a murderer, but she could not be sure. She sensed that even Angie was not completely sure. She decided that it was not prudent to rule Marcus out, just because he was one of the most likely suspects. Sometimes it turned out that the most likely suspect was the perpetrator—quite often, in fact, from her experience.

Of course, it could have been Tony.

Tony admitted to having been at the Manor on Tuesday and admitted stealing money from his parents' room. As a matter of fact, Tony was emerging as the media favorite, the most likely suspect, surpassing Marcus, according to the morning news. His estrangement from his father and his desperate need for money fell right in line with the most common motives for murder. After all, most murders are committed by relatives or friends, and Tony's story lacked the ring of truth. He had been caught in a lie, which reduced his credibility to a point somewhere below zero.

Who else?

The air of suspicion surrounding Randy could not be ruled out. Was he who he said he was? Or was Chantal right about there being something not just right about him?

That left the rest of the staff. Ernie, Chantal, the maids, Christa, Peter, and Erika. Or an unknown intruder from outside.

Having sifted the evidence as much as she could, Molly grabbed a quick breakfast of coffee and a buttered biscuit, then stopped at the flower shop on the main street and began to study each bouquet displayed in buckets in front of the store. Finally she selected a small bunch of brightly colored blossoms that fit her pocketbook, paid the clerk, and headed off down the street to the rack where her bicycle was parked. Off she rode back to the spa, a miniature black butterfly accompanying her almost half the way, no doubt attracted by the radiant blooms in her basket.

Meanwhile, the sky had begun to darken, and the air felt moist. By the time she turned off the main road onto the lane leading to the manor, large raindrops were beginning to fall.

Reverend Stromb, who was sitting on the covered front porch of his house, saw her predicament and called out to her. "Come and get out of the rain!"

Sliding off the seat of the bicycle, she pushed it up the driveway incline as she called out, "Good morning, Reverend! Thanks for the offer; I'll take you up on it!"

Dale stood up to greet her and said, "Looks like just a brief cloud burst. It'll be over in a few minutes. My name's Stromb, Dale Stromb."

"Nice to meet you, Revered Stromb; Mr. Snale has mentioned you. I'm Molly May. As you may know, I'm one of the guests at Clareton Manor. I've just taken a ride to town to get a bit of relief from the terrible tension at the Manor. You know what happened, I'm sure?"

"Yes, I'm afraid I do, Mrs. May," Dale responded, shaking his head. "I have lived in the town all my life, and never has anything like this happened here." Actually he was glad to have the chance to get more inside news about the incident. Very little had been reported on the television or in the newspaper; wealthy people were often able to curtail unwanted publicity, even in death. "This sudden rainstorm has interrupted a week of otherwise beautiful weather, hasn't it?" He was trying to make small talk, something he specialized in.

"Oh, my, yes, but April showers are required to bring May flowers, aren't they?" Molly smiled sweetly.

"The rain will make the lane muddy, though. Not good when you're on foot."

"And the murder has muddied the air, so we have mud above and below, don't we?"

"Terrible, terrible incident. One hardly knows what to think. As trite as it sounds, it's hard not to say that things like this never happen in Clareton." Dale was pushing forward a wicker chair for Molly to sit in. "There's been so little in the news—have the police made an arrest?" He was trying to sound casual.

Molly pretended not to notice anything else in his tone. "No, they haven't. As far as I can tell, they are nowhere near an arrest. There are several suspects, but no real evidence to support any theory" Molly was unusually frank; she wanted to encourage him to talk, to find out what he might have heard from his sources, especially Ernie. "Actually I suppose all of us are suspects. It's unlikely that anyone from the outside could have entered the Manor grounds unseen. For that matter, an intruder would likely have passed by your cottage here and might have been seen by you."

"Unless he sneaked through the woods," Dale responded, not knowing whether or not she knew about the interview he had had with Officer Windham about the blue Toyota. After a little thought, he decided there was nothing to be gained by withholding the information from her. "I did see a blue Toyota pass by on Tuesday afternoon. The police asked me about it. I don't know if it's significant. They didn't say."

By then the sky had darkened ominously, and the wind was gusting. A sudden lightning bolt accompanied by a thunderous roar startled them both.

"Mrs. May," said Dale, "I'm afraid you'll have to sit here a bit longer—you can't go out in this storm."

"I'm so sorry to trouble you like this, Reverend." Molly tilted her head to one side and looked at Dale with the saddest eyes she could call to duty.

"No trouble at all, Ma'am. I'm glad for the company. I get few visitors, except for Ernie Snale, of course."

"Ernie visits often, does he?"

"Oh, yes, at least once a day when he's working. He doesn't feel comfortable taking a break over at the Manor, and when he feels the need for a rest, he drops by where he can relax out of sight." Dale chuckled a little. He knew how Ernie hated to work and sought out places to hide where he would not be detected if he napped a little. Truth be told, it was the extra day labor that Mrs. Bischoff hired that got most of the landscaping done. He wasn't sure why Mrs. Bischoff kept Ernie on the payroll, unless she was just reluctant to "upset the apple cart," so to speak.

"He seems like a pleasant enough fellow. And the landscaping is lovely." Molly knew that honey caught more flies than vinegar, so she spread it thick.

"Well," Dale responded, slowly measuring his words, "Ernie's a friend of mine and all, but I don't think there's anyone who would credit him with the way the place looks. He's a fine, friendly fellow, but a lazier one I've never seen."

"You seem to know him well. Have you known him long?" Molly asked. She continued to act in a nonchalant manner, surveying the sky as she spoke, but her ears were perked up for any clue that might be forthcoming.

"Most of my life," Dale answered. He leaned back in his rocking chair and looked off to one side. He knew he should hold his tongue, but Mrs. May seemed like a dotty old lady who could do him no harm. "Actually, I grew up in the Manor House—it belonged to my grandfather Akin, my maternal grandfather. I was born in the house; my folks lived with my grandparents. There was plenty of room, even then, before Erika added the new wing. Ernie's father was the gardener then; his family lived in the little cook's cottage. So we grew up together."

"How wonderful!" Molly gushed. "So, at some point you sold the house and moved up here, into something, shall we say, more suitable?"

"No, it didn't happen like that at all. After my grand-daddy died, my mother inherited the estate. It didn't take long for my father to lose it all. He loved the spirits and the casinos quite a lot, and women too. He ran up debt, mortgaged the house, and when he couldn't cover the payments, the bank eventually foreclosed. It was sold at auction a long time ago. I was still a child, not quite a teenager yet. We moved to town to a shabby rented apartment. By the time I graduated from

Seminary, both my parents had died. I applied for the pastorate of the Sweetwater Church here in Clareton, and I got the job. It doesn't pay much; that may be why there was so little competition for the job. I saved up to make a down payment on this place. I can't see the Manor House from here, but I know it's there. Sometimes I sit here on the porch and reminisce about the old days. Ernie keeps me informed on how things look and what changes have been made."

Molly felt bad and didn't quite know what to say. "I'm sorry, Dale. I didn't know. I didn't mean to pry."

"That's okay, Mrs. May." Dale smiled. "It doesn't matter now. Maybe knowing the history will help to make my friendship with Ernie a little easier to understand. We really don't have much in common, except the Manor House." He sounded a little wistful. "It was almost mine."

"Finally it's letting up," Molly said as she tilted her head to look under the porch roof at the sky. "Let me be on my way and let you return to what you were doing." As she descended the porch steps, she noticed a mature rose bush in the corner between the steps and porch; it had a couple of buds and a drooping bloom or two. It was badly in need of pruning. Yet Dale sat on his porch day after day, not ten feet away from the despairing bush, refusing to tend to its needs. That was evidence to support the theory that laziness feeds upon itself and continues to self-propagate, she thought. The less one does, the less one wants to do. The old adage "idleness is the devil's workshop" popped into her head too, but that was a different issue.

"Drop by any time, Mrs. May," replied the Reverend, standing. "Nice to meet you. I enjoyed your visit."

"Nice to meet you too." Molly waved as she dried off the seat of the bicycle with a tissue from her pocket. "See you later!" She was pleased to note the rain had kept the flowers she had bought from wilting during her visit with the Reverend.

Molly's agile brain began to analyze the Reverend Dale Stromb without any prompting. His friendliness was charming, yet he seemed a little manipulative, his charm egotistical in a way she couldn't really explain. His nonchalant manner when he talked about losing the Manor House puzzled her. She had seen that cocky manner displayed by countless criminals she had interviewed over the years—it was a kind of unwillingness to accept responsibility for anything. There's something good and something bad in everyone, or almost everyone, but there were some people who were totally devoid of empathy toward others—sociopaths, they were called. Oh, stop, Molly, she thought to herself. You're always analyzing everyone and everything. You know how annoying that can be! Her attention turned to her surroundings as she turned the bicycle around in the driveway to face the lane.

A glance downward to locate the kick stand on the bicycle to release it fixed on a little patch of dandelions. She picked up her leg to climb onto the bicycle and noticed a prickly dandelion seed attached to her pant leg. She pulled it off and thought what interesting creatures dandelion seeds are. On one end, they are soft and fluffy and cling to you; on the other end they are tough and sharp and pierce you. There was a clump of dandelions by the driveway; some were still yellow and others had already gone to seed.

Part V

Persistence Pays

26

Back at the Manor

Arriving back at the spa, as she was putting the bicycle, still dripping from the heavy downpour, back in its assigned place, Molly felt the presence of another person. Gathering up her bouquet of spring flowers, she turned to face an attractive young woman with a hangdog expression on her face and a slightly unkempt appearance, as if she had had less than an adequate night's sleep.

"Good morning," said Molly to the bedraggled young woman, pretending not to notice her untidy appearance. "Looks like it might turn out to be a nice day after the morning storm."

"Good morning. Yes, it does. The air is starting to feel cleaner already," Cindy replied as politely as she could in spite of her inward tension. She tossed her head as if feeling the air.

Sensing her unease, Molly shifted her flowers into her left arm, and reached out her right hand. "My name is Molly May; I'm one of the guests here at the spa."

Cindy extended her hand to meet Molly's. "Nice to meet you, Molly. I'm Cindy Caruthers. I'm a friend of Tony's. Tony's the . . ."

"Of course. Tony Ruger. I'm so sorry about what happened."

"Me too. Tony is very upset, just devastated. And his mother too, of course."

"I understand you and Tony flew up from New Orleans yesterday?"

"Yes, we did. We arrived yesterday afternoon. Tony has spent most of the time with his mother since we've been here. His mother and the cops."

"And you've been left alone."

Cindy looked up for the first time and let out a heavy sigh. "Yes, alone and lonely too."

"Would you like someone to talk to? If so, I'm available."

Cindy replied in the affirmative. She had heard that Molly had been a police detective with the Columbia police department—and a very good one.

"How long have you known Tony?" Molly asked as they walked toward the front of the house.

"Only a couple of months, actually. He's a friendly, outgoing guy, lots of fun to be around. He never meets a stranger, as they say. I suppose I fell for him right away."

"I suppose you had no chance to meet his parents before now."

"You're exactly right. I didn't know much about them except that they were wealthy, and Tony got checks from his mother on a regular basis. He didn't talk much about his father, but I knew they weren't close."

"So, is this your first trip to South Carolina?"

Cindy hesitated. She tried to remember what Tony had said he told the police about his trip to Clareton on Tuesday. Did they know she was with him? She didn't want to contradict his story; that might make things worse when the papers were already hinting at links between his visit to Clareton and his father's murder.

"Yes, . . . I mean, no. I've been here before. Once or twice."

Molly decided to be direct and ask the question that was on her mind. "Was one of those times this past Tuesday?"

"Okay, yes. I hesitated before I answered because I didn't know if Tony had told the police or not," she admitted, ashamed of how easy it seemed to lie. "He didn't want me to be involved in this mess. We were in desperate need of money. The rent hadn't been paid, and we were about to be evicted. Tony isn't thrifty like I am, and he had frittered away the money his mother sent him for living expenses. He needed more money and was ashamed to admit to her that he had wasted the money she sent—he bought another digital camera—he already had one, but he wanted a fancier one—more mega pixels. There went the rent money. We were about to be put out on the street. We drove up from New Orleans, so that Tony could beg her to get him out of the predicament he'd gotten himself into. He thought a face-to-face contact would be more likely to sway her. I waited in the car while Tony went inside to talk to his mother." Cindy was amazed at her ability to stretch the truth; part of the story she told was half-true—they did need money, but that wasn't the reason for the trip. At least, it wasn't the reason Tony had given her; she thought it would be best to keep her story consistent with the one Tony had told the police. Nothing was said about the side trip to Spartanburg.

"How unfortunate for you to have come here on the very day that Harvey Ruger was murdered!"

"A lot of people are saying that it was more than a coincidence. Especially the Clareton newspaper."

"How do you feel about that?"

"Just awful. I know Tony didn't kill his father." Then she added, "He told me he didn't, and I believe him."

"I hope you don't mind my saying so, but you don't sound completely convinced of that."

"It's hard to be certain about something you didn't witness personally, even though you know and trust a person, isn't it?"

"Yes, I suppose so. I know how you feel. Even when a person has an impeccable reputation, when something like this happens, it can cause suspicion."

"I wouldn't want to believe anything bad about Tony. Especially something criminal." She couldn't say, "Murder;" she could barely think it.

"If he had committed a crime, do you think he could conceal it from you?"

"I feel almost certain he could not. He's very expressive, an extrovert if ever there was one. He's very open with everyone; he loves to share himself. His main fault is his irresponsibility with money and the fundamental necessities of life. He has never learned the meaning of the word 'thrifty,' and he would give his last five dollar bill to someone he saw in need. On the other hand, he expects others to do the same for him, and they rarely do, . . . except for his mother, of course. Coming from a wealthy family has played a part in that, I'm sure, but I think being happy-go-lucky is in his genes too."

"So, deep down you really don't believe Tony was involved in his father's death."

"You're right; I don't. I think there's something else he's not telling me, but I'm not sure what it is.

"Let's hold on to the hope that justice will prevail."

About that time they heard the lunch bell ring, so they went inside. Molly hurriedly took the flowers up to her room to put them in water and then rushed back downstairs to the dining room to join the others who had already gathered there.

For lunch Randy had prepared a thick, rich and delicious lentil soup. It was a Middle Eastern staple that he had known from childhood. With warm, homemade bread and a salad of freshly-picked greens, the soup made a comforting meal, perfect for warming the body and soul.

Before lunch was over, Molly began to feel uncomfortable in her damp clothes, a result of being caught in the rainstorm during her morning outing, so as soon as she finished her soup, she excused herself and went to her room for a quick shower and some dry clothes. She changed into a pair of comfortable light cotton slacks and a pale green t-shirt. Back downstairs on her way out, she stopped by Christa's outer office to sign up for a massage. There was only one available appointment left for the day on Christa's schedule—at 4:30 P.M. She wrote her name in. Glancing at Barry's schedule, she noticed it was blank. Odd, she thought. She went looking for company but saw no one except Chantal and the two maids in the kitchen. She waved at them but didn't stop.

She walked out onto the front porch and still saw no one. Assuming that the other guests were secluded in their rooms or in the hot tubs, she elected a brief stroll to balance the hearty lunch she'd had. Not up to running into Reverend Stromb twice on the same day, she turned in the opposite direction and followed the unpaved pathway around to the rear of the house. Soon she could hear the tinkling of wind chimes as she approached the little cook's cottage.

Randy's little cottage seemed as serene as it had the day she visited him there. The path wound close around the side of the cottage. As she neared the open kitchen window, she stopped suddenly as she heard voices and ducked her head low. She held her breath; it was Randy speaking with someone whose voice she recognized as one she had heard recently—Dale Stromb! What would he be doing here? she puzzled. It never occurred to her that the two men might be acquainted; Dale had told her about his long friendship with Ernie but did not mention even a passing acquaintance with Randy. For that matter, he had given her the impression that the only knowledge he had of the manor and its grounds was through Ernie. Debating whether to reveal her presence to them or to retreat in silence, she felt a surge of the old investigative instinct within her. She listened for a while and then took a couple of silent steps backward, turned and strode back up the hill toward the Manor House.

She went to her room and spent some time in silence, watching the gentle wafting of the leafy boughs outside her window. The formal activities with paid instructors had been cancelled for the rest of the week. Just as well, she thought.

The group tension would work against any attempt at relaxation.

In spite of herself, Molly replayed the events and the evidence related to Harvey's murder in her mind most of the afternoon. She tried different ways of fitting the piece of Dale and Randy together into the overall puzzle, but she wasn't quite able to see the whole picture. "I need the box cover," she thought to herself. But maybe the piece didn't go into this puzzle at all.

Detective Bloom and Officer Windham did not come back to the house that day, although they sent uniformed officers to pick up Tony and take him downtown for further interrogation. Molly watched out her bedroom window as they led him away. Something didn't feel right about the scene—she felt sorry for Tony, even if he was a lazy, irresponsible fellow. There were plenty of ne'er-do-well's who don't find themselves hauled off downtown to be questioned about murdering their sires. Though she didn't know Tony and hadn't had a chance to talk to him herself, there was a aura of honesty about Cindy. Cindy wasn't positive that Tony was innocent, but her sensibilities pointed in that direction. Molly liked to go with the expert in a matter, so she leaned toward Cindy's judgment in this case. For now anyway.

"Oh, well," she sighed out loud. "It's not coming to me now." Turning her attention away from the crime, she donned a simple, conservative swimsuit and headed for an afternoon dip in the hot springs tub, followed by an extended massage. That would unwind Molly's springs.

The massage, a visit with Erika, a quick supper, and some light television rounded out the day. She chose ancient sitcom reruns over the news; she knew too much about what was going on already.

27
Breakfast in Bed

When Molly awoke on Friday, the sun was already indicating mid-morning. She looked at the clock; it was 9:30 A.M. She couldn't remember when she had slept that late, but she still felt too tired to move. Then she realized that she'd just had the first solid night's sleep since Sunday. No wonder she was so tired.

She was sure she'd already missed breakfast, so she rang the main desk and asked Christa, who answered the ring, to send coffee up to her room. Christa replied that some excellent fresh, free-range hen eggs had been delivered that morning and asked if she wouldn't like a proper breakfast with eggs and biscuits. Becoming aware of her morning hunger, Molly accepted.

As she began her morning rituals of physical and spiritual exercise, Molly's mind sorted through the clues or possible clues, that had presented so far. It occurred to her that she had forgotten to ask Christa why Barry's appointment schedule was blank the day before. Soon she found herself seated in a cross-legged position, with all activity and thought suspended.

A gentle tapping at the door interrupted her silence. It was Christa with a huge, steaming breakfast. Molly smiled at the sight of her.

"Hmmm. That smells good!" Molly said. "But if I eat all that, I'll look even more like I'm trying to conceal a football under my shirt."

"Nonsense, Aunt Molly," laughed Christa. You look great for a woman your age."

"You could have left off the 'your age' part, dear," Molly responded teasingly.

"I can't disagree with that, Auntie." Christa set the breakfast tray on the little round table with the lace-trimmed tablecloth under the east window. "I hope you enjoy it," said Christa, starting to exit the room.

"Oh, wait, Christa. I meant to ask you about something yesterday afternoon, and I forgot."

"What's that?"

"When I signed up for a massage yesterday with you, I noticed that Barry's appointment schedule was blank. It seemed odd to me that he wouldn't have any clients yesterday."

"You didn't know? Barry didn't show up for work yesterday. Mom called his apartment repeatedly for hours and got no answer, so she called the police. He's gone. Cleared out. The police have an APB out on him."

"Gone! Oh, dear me!"

"Doesn't look good for Barry, does it?"

"I don't know what to say! I didn't expect this!"

"Nor did I. I hope he has a good explanation for it. See you later, Aunt Molly." Christa went out and closed the door behind her, leaving Molly to her steaming breakfast.

The breakfast was a real treat, and Molly relished every bite. The aroma of the eggs reminded her of the old days on the farm when the eggs were really good and fresh. Factory-farm eggs from caged hens who spent their entire lives in a space of one half a square foot were tasteless; she didn't know why. Meantime, there was freshly-made soy sausage spiced with an expert hand. The biscuits were hot and homey, not doughy like those at the fast-food eateries she had frequented when she was on the police force. On the side were fresh strawberries, shipped upstate from the low country, where they were just beginning to ripen. The coffee was excellent. She was fond of joking that coffee was the only reason she got up in the morning; this coffee was good enough to entice anyone out of bed.

Once breakfast was over, she dressed in a sweatshirt and jeans. When she cracked a window to get some fresh air, the coldness caused her to shut it again quickly. The weather on that Friday was a dramatic change from the earlier part of the week; a cold front had passed through overnight, consistent with April's changeable nature. The morning was foggy and gray, and by mid-morning, it was raining steadily. There was a dampness about. She realized the reason her room felt warm was that Erika had turned the heat on. When she got downstairs, she saw flames in the gas-log fireplaces in the parlor and dining room. She went looking for Erika and found her in her office, glasses low on her nose, and her fingers flying at the computer keyboard.

When Erika saw her, she stopped her furious typing and sat back in the chair. "Good morning, my friend. Up early this morning, aren't we?" It was approaching eleven o'clock.

Chuckling at the friendly jab, Molly replied, "I can't tell you how tired I was. I feel great now after the sumptuous breakfast Christa served."

"I'm glad you got some rest. I was beginning to worry about you."

"It turned cool last night, didn't it? I noticed the heat was on."

"Yes, it did. Just one more bill – one more headache."

"I'm so sorry, poor Erika. May I intrude for a few minutes? I need to talk to you about some things."

She sat down, and they talked intently for some time. Finally Erika nodded approval to something Molly had said, and Molly got up to leave. "I'll let you know what I find out," she said.

She walked through the parlor and then to the kitchen, making polite small talk with guests and staff she met on her way. In the kitchen, she found Randy preparing lunch.

"Good morning, Randy," she said. "I was wondering if perhaps I could get another cup of that delicious coffee."

"Of course. I'll get it for you." He took a mug from the cupboard and poured it for her.

"Thanks. Hot coffee is so good on a cold day. Or any day, for that matter," she laughed.

Randy mumbled a reply and continued with his meal preparations. So she went on, saying, "Erika tells me you're going away for the weekend. We'll miss your fine cooking if we have to stay on."

"Very kind of you to say so. Actually, Mrs. Bischoff asked me to come back as soon as I can if any of the guests are still here after today," Randy replied. "I can go to Columbia and pick up some things I'll need and bring them back here to work on this weekend. If I leave right after I finish preparing lunch, I'll be back in time to prepare a simple supper. I'll send Chantal for provisions; she enjoys going to town to the market. She runs into her friends, and they have a grand time spreading the latest gossip."

"Please have a safe trip. Traffic seems to get worse and worse all the time. I hope to see you when you get back."

"I'll be careful. If all goes well, I'll see you tonight. Goodbye, Ms. May."

Holding her coffee cup in both hands, she wandered to the parlor and sat in a chair by the window and chatted casually with some of the other guests until she saw Randy's car head down the lane. Retrieving a jacket from her room, she eased into the kitchen. She selected a large umbrella from the stand near the back door and nonchalantly headed down the path toward the cottage, as if on a mere exercise outing.

28
Cottage Clues

With Randy away, she would have a chance to get into the cottage and look around. She wanted to know why Dale had been there the day before with Randy. She had caught only snatches of the conversation and hoped to be able to find something to fill in some of the missing pieces. She did not know what she was looking for, but she was sure she would recognize it when she saw it.

When she reached the cottage, she continued around the path to the kitchen door. By now the rain had slacked off to a sprinkle, but the air was damp and chilly. The door was locked, but she noticed that the window was still open, just a crack—the same window that had allowed her to hear the startling combination of voices the day before. She wanted to look around for some clue that might explain Dale's presence there. A cursory examination confirmed that the window screen was merely pressed into the window frame; there was no latch. A little fingernail file from the dainty lady's pocketknife she always carried pried it off with little effort. An empty clay flowerpot awaiting some spring planting near the back steps made an adequate stool when overturned. She was glad she was wearing her most comfortable pair of jeans as she contorted herself to get through the opening. At fifty-five she was still wiry and flexible enough to do it, thanks to faithful yoga practice and weight training.

She slid to the floor inside the kitchen; her sleuthing background was still fairly fresh, and it rose quickly to attention. What she was looking for, she did not know: any clue could present a string to pull. Her experienced eyes poured methodically over every inch in the kitchen and then the living room, bedroom, and bath. Nothing was out of the ordinary.

Returning to the kitchen, she sat on a stool to rest and to think. Her eyes drifted slowly downward; she caught herself thinking that the softwood floors in these old houses were lovely. The nesting instinct was one feminine trait she had plenty of; houses and everything associated with them held an endless fascination for her.

She slid a languorous foot over the plank floor, as if to admire it through the sense of touch; the soft edge of her shoe sole caught on something. She repeated the maneuver and experienced the same tug. Fairly bounding off the stool, she crouched on her hands and knees, and felt the floor surface with her hands.

Carefully concealed in the architecture and partially concealed by the kitchen table was a trap door. She slid the table aside and found a smoothly rounded countersunk bolt head in the door. Using her fingernail file again, she was able to raise the bolt head high enough to grasp it. In response to her pull, the door began to creak and open.

I wonder what's down here, she thought to herself. Maybe an old cellar for food storage?— apples and potatoes and such? The ladder leading into the cellar was in good shape, no doubt replaced in the recent past. She looked around for a flashlight and found a small one with a bright light in a basket on the counter near the door. Then she climbed down the stairs to take a look around the cellar. On one end of the cellar was an opening to a passageway. Using her small light, she set out to find where it went, hoping she could get back before she was discovered.

It was a long, winding pathway. The floor was smooth and seemed to be made of some kind of stone tile. There were ancient beams spaced along the sides of the walls with shelves and cabinets lining them. The only odor was that of cool damp earth; no fresh produce had been stored here for a very long time. On some of the wooden shelves were old canning jars, some filled, and bottles and cans. Half wondering if she had stumbled on to nothing more than a 1950s-era bomb shelter, she did not stop to examine anything on the way; she first wanted to find what was at the other end.

She picked her way carefully—the small flashlight shone only a few feet ahead. At the end there was a wooden ladder leading up to another trap door at the other end. The ladder did not look any older than the one she had come down. She climbed up the ladder, minding to be as quiet as possible, and opened the door the tiniest crack. "Oh, dear me!" she breathed quietly to herself. She found herself under the small utility room off the back porch of the Manor House, near the back stairs! A secret passageway! Who knew about it? she wondered. It was odd that it was still intact after all these years—the original house was well over one hundred years old. She felt certain that it had been used in recent years; someone had replaced the ladder stairway at both ends for one thing.

Molly felt as though she had stumbled upon an important secret, but she wasn't sure what it meant in regard to the ongoing investigation into Harvey Ruger's murder, if anything. It was another entrance to the Manor House, but there was only one entrance to the tunnel that she could see. If a yet undiscovered intruder had entered the house by the tunnel, he or she would have had to enter through the cook's cottage. Remembering how easy it had been for her to gain access to the cottage with Randy away, she supposed anyone might have slipped in. For that matter, it could have been someone off the main road. Crime was rampant these days; as a former member of the police department, she knew only too well how little effort went into apprehending petty thieves and burglars. Even if they were caught, the courts usually turned them loose, so why bother? So it was not really much of a stretch to include a random thief as a suspect in the Ruger murder, especially after finding this clandestine entrance.

Not wanting to be discovered by anyone, she let the trap door lid slide shut very softly and began to tread softly back through the tunnel. She walked slowly, pausing frequently, and examined her surroundings for what she knew not. Her closer examination indicated that the tunnel was still in use. There was loose dirt on the path, making it easy to see the many footprints going in both directions. The tunnel was still in frequent use. By whom and for what?

As she neared the end of the tunnel, she slowed her pace and strained her ears for any sound at all. She heard nothing. Entering Randy's kitchen through the trapdoor, she put everything back the way she found it; she wiped off scuff marks from the trap door and pulled the table back into its position, matching the base of the table legs inside their faint dust marks. She put the flashlight back into the basket and checked to make sure the position was just as she found it. Since the door had a simple lock that could be locked from within and then just pulled shut from outside, she decided to go out that way. She pulled the window back down, leaving it open just the tiny crack she had found. Once outside, she put the screen back into the kitchen window and the flower pot back where she found it by the back stair steps. Then, she hastily fled back to the Manor House.

29
Cobwebs

She considered her options and decided she would have to confide in Erika in order to find out more about the secret passageway and what it was being used for. Not finding Erika, Molly went looking for Christa instead. Erika was out, at the insurance agent's office, Christa said, trying to find out if her business insurance would help to cover the losses of the week. Standing in the outer waiting area of the massage therapy suite, Christa leaned over and lifted a piece of cobweb off Molly's head.

"We don't usually see cobwebs like these until the fall of year, Aunt Molly. Where have you been? Under the bed?" laughed Christa.

"No, not exactly under the bed," Molly replied, wondering whether or not to reveal her discovery to Christa. "But under something, for sure."

"Oh, you mean the tunnel? How did you find that?"

"Tunnel? What tunnel?" Molly thought keeping her options open for the moment might be the best course of action.

"Underground passageway might be a better term. Actually, Randy is the only one who uses it anymore. I didn't know anyone used it until one day when I was on the back porch, taking a break with Barry, I saw Randy coming up the path. It startled me because when we first went out onto the porch, Randy was in the kitchen, and he didn't go to the cottage by way of the path—from where we were standing, the path was in full view, and we would have seen anyone on it. I joked to Barry that it must be some sort of Eastern magic—sort of like levitation. When I got a chance to ask Randy about it, he at first tried to deny it and then just tried to blow me off.

"So later that day, I checked it out, and, sure enough, it was still passable from the cottage to the utility room here in the big house. We had heard stories about it from the servants, but we never paid much attention to them. Thought it was just fantasy. They said it was used in plantation days by the house slaves to sneak away to their shacks for a reprieve while the gentry sipped mint juleps on the front porch. Chantal said her grandmother used to tell the story of her forebears slipping through the tunnel many times on hot summer afternoons. They assumed it was full of rats and snakes and probably caved in by now, so they never tried to go down there. When I saw Randy appear as if by magic, coming up the path without going down it first, I checked it out. I got Peter and Barry to go with me; I didn't know what we might run into to. We found that it was passable all the way from the cottage to the big house— and not in too bad shape either."

"Why use the tunnel for a mundane trip to the cottage?" wondered Molly.

"Maybe just to play a trick on us. Are you sleuthing, Aunt Molly?"

"Just between you and me, Christa, yes, I am."

"Found any useful clues yet?"

"Not that I know of. At least nothing that seems to lead anywhere. Who else knows about the tunnel?"

"No one, I guess. Peter and I didn't even mention it to Mother. Didn't think she would be interested. When I was a child, she laughed at my devotion to Trixie Belden mystery stories; the tunnel reminded me of some of those books. She never showed any interest in 'whodunits'. So I didn't bother to discuss it with her."

"Interesting," said Molly. She didn't bother to mention the shoe-print evidence in the tunnel that indicated it was a frequently used route. And there was evidence of more than one shoe size too. Of course, Christa had just said that she, Peter, and Barry had all been in the tunnel, so that could account for it, she supposed. According to Reverend Stromb, Ernie had lived in the cook's cottage when he was a boy. He must know about the tunnel. For that matter, Dale would know too, since the two of them played together as children. She decided to ask Ernie about it. Even if he uttered nothing more than his usual rude response, she might be able to learn something by his expression when he found out that she knew about it.

"Christa, thanks for clearing the cobwebs out of my head," Molly laughed. "I must be going. The afternoon will be gone, and I won't have completed my hot tub or my yoga!"

"Or your massage, Aunt Molly. Now please don't forget your massage; you know how it helps you sleep."

"I'll see you at four-thirty sharp; it's become my regular time—I won't forget!" called Molly behind her as she hurried off, her lean, lanky figure striding rapidly away.

30
Ernie Snale

Finding Ernie took a little effort; he was asleep behind the potting shed in an old, faded canvas beach chair, arms dangling down on either side of him.

"Excuse me, Mr. Snale! Didn't mean to bother you. A bit cool and damp this afternoon, isn't it?"

The sound of her voice made Ernie jump nearly out of the chair. "Thought you was Miz Bischoff," was the only greeting she got, and a groggy one at that.

"Oh, no. I was out for a walk, exploring a little. Christa said there was an old underground passageway around here somewhere. It has some history associated with it, I understand. I'm a real history buff," she gushed. "You don't know where it is, do you?"

Ernie's face brightened, and he looked as though he was about to launch into a full disclosure, but then he caught himself. He loved to show off his knowledge, what there was of it, but Mrs. May wasn't "in the club," so to speak, so he decided to keep her in the dark as much as he could.

"I don' know wha'cha talkin' about. If Christa knows so much about it, ask her."

Molly decided it was time to press on with the interrogation. Ernie may be hostile, but he wasn't especially bright. She ought to be able to get something out of him. "But you lived here when you were a child growing up, didn't you? Didn't you play in the tunnel as a child?"

"Who tole you that?" demanded Ernie, watching her out of squinted eyes, his face tight with animosity. He had not risen from the chair, but his position was now askew, as a result of the sudden awakening.

"Why, I believe it was Reverend Stromb, now that you mention it." Molly was smiling her sweetest smile.

"Dale? Dale Stromb tole you that? He must be mistaken." Ernie was looking around furtively, looking for an exit route.

"Not exactly. What he did say was that when he lived in the Manor House with his grandparents, you and your folks lived in the cottage. Said the two of you were best friends as children and played together."

"Even if we did, 'at don' mean we played in any tunnel. An' I ain't sayin' there is one."

"There is one, Ernie. You know it, and I know it now too. What I'm wondering is why you don't want to talk about it."

"Maybe it ain't the 'what' but the 'who' in this conversation that's buggin' me." With that he stormed off, his rapid pace making his dangling arms flail about him.

Then I'll go back to Dale's house, thought Molly. Persistence will get to the bottom of this.

As she approached Dale's house, she heard Ernie's whiney voice as the front screened door slammed shut. Ernie had the same idea she had and had arrived ahead of her. She crept near the house and listened at an open window. I mustn't let this become a habit, she thought. Ernie was talking rapidly and loudly in his excitement. Soon she had the information she needed, and she sneaked back down the lane to the big house.

31
Tunnel Trip Two

Based on the discussion she overhead at Dale's house, she knew now where to look for the evidence she needed. It was in the tunnel. She glanced at her watch. Did she have time to get it today before Randy got back from Columbia? No sooner had the thought flashed through her mind than she knew she had to try. There was too much at stake; delay would only give the perpetrators involved time to remove the evidence. There wasn't time to call Detective Bloom. Besides, if she was wrong, she didn't want the police to know about it. No one was around; all was still and quiet.

She set out for the cottage at a brisk pace. Once there, she quickly repeated her previous break-in and twisted her wiry body through the kitchen window. This time she went out the back door, replaced the screen on the window so that if anyone came while she was there, her entrance would not be noticed, and reentered the back door, locking it behind her. If Randy got back before she was finished, she could wait for the right opportunity when she would not be seen and exit at the Manor House utility room.

Wasting no time, she was back in the tunnel, flashlight in hand, with the trap door closed above her. Once inside there was no way she could move the table back, but with nothing else amiss, if Randy got back before she could get out, maybe he would assume that he had left the table out of place himself.

With little trouble, she found the cabinet doors that had come up in Ernie's anxious conversation with Dale a short time earlier. There was no lock. Molly opened both doors at once and drew them back. The flashlight beam fell on the contents: loot of various descriptions—jewelry, watches, electronics and greenbacks, lots of it. She took out her cell phone and tried to call Detective Bloom, but the signal could not get through the earthen surroundings. She wished she had taken the time to call earlier.

She flicked the phone shut and slipped it into her pocket. Then closing the doors, she saw the light of another flashlight coming down the passageway. She thought about turning hers off to try to conceal herself, until she knew who it was, but it was too late. She'd been seen. Instead, she turned her flashlight directly into the face of the intruder.

It was Dale. She was relieved to see that Ernie was not with him. Dale appeared to be levelheaded, whatever else he might be; but Ernie was unpredictable.

"Dale!" she said. "Oh, dear me, but you frightened me!"

"What are you doing here?"

"I could ask you the same thing."

"Did you find what you were looking for?" Dale ignored her response and pressed on with his question.

She couldn't see his eyes but his voice was dark and hard. "Yes, I did. Why don't you tell me what you know about this."

"What makes you think I know anything about it?"

"You're here, aren't you? I overhead your conversation with Ernie a little while ago." She recounted the discussion she had had with Ernie, how she had then proceeded to Dale's house to try to understand why Ernie had been so intimidated by her questions, and how she had discovered that Ernie had arrived ahead of her.

"Being a nosy busybody is not a christian trait. Could get you into trouble."

"One could say the same thing about stealing. Let's go outside and discuss this sensibly."

"No, let's stay here. We'll talk about it here." He motioned with his light to some old wooden crates by the wall. "Sit down."

32
We've Got a Problem

Molly's nerves were in a heightened state of alertness, and she was attuned to every nuance of his body language. She'd been in some tight places before, but never without a gun, as she was now. What was going on in his mind? How extensive was this theft ring? Was he in so deeply involved that he might feel the need to silence her? After all, he was a minister, a man of the cloth. Few churches would retain a pastor who was convicted of burglary. If he were found out, he would certainly lose his job as well as his position in his hometown society. Did this have anything to do with the murder of Harvey Ruger? If so, had one of them done it? Or did they know who had?

As they sat down, footsteps were heard in the deep blackness of the tunnel. "That you, Dale?" a voice called out. Another person to deal with; Molly's tension increased. As he got nearer, she realized to her relief it wasn't Ernie; it was Randy. He soon appeared in the dim light of their two flashlights.

"Hey, Randy. We've got a problem," Dale said, nodding in Molly's direction.

"Mrs. May!" Randy exclaimed. "Whatever are you doing here? How did you get here?"

187

"Never mind that. Will you two please tell me what this is all about." She said "please," but she used her most authoritative voice, and there was no question mark punctuating her demand.

"Maybe it would be better for you, if you didn't know." It was Randy speaking, plaintively. He seemed miserable that Molly had gotten involved in their affairs this way.

"Randy, I saw jewelry and cash and various other trinkets in the wall cabinet. A lot of it. You don't have to be in the police business to know stolen property when you see it. There's no other reason for it to be here. And I heard Ernie talking to Dale about it. The police will have to know. I've got to tell them what I've seen and heard." She decided to tell them that she had already called Bloom; it was true, though the call had not gone through; it was always best not to tell everything you know. That was one of the few rules of life that held at least ninety-nine per cent of the time.

Now Randy addressed Dale directly. "She's right, you know. We've been discovered, and we may as well face our punishment."

"Easy for you to say. You're not putting your livelihood at stake. I have done nothing in my life but pastor a church. I have no other skills. Once I'm arrested, I'll be kicked out of the church immediately. At my age it's too late for me to learn anything else. With a robbery conviction on my record, I couldn't even get a job as a grocery store clerk. Come on, Randy; work with me on this," Dale pleaded.

Molly was dumbfounded at his directness but also relieved that Dale hadn't mentioned murder. She didn't know if there was any connection, but she was sure the time to find out was not while she was trapped in the tunnel without a weapon and with the two potentially dangerous men. Her feeling at the moment, however, was that she would rather be trapped with robbers than murderers.

"I suppose you robbed Harvey Ruger," she said quietly, not looking at either of them.

"Absolutely not," replied Randy. "We hadn't had the chance by the time he was killed."

"So you were planning to."

"He was a rich man. He would not miss a twenty dollar bill."

"What if I told you the police have evidence that you were there on the day he was murdered?"

"I'd say you were being less than honest, Mrs. May," Randy replied.

"What evidence?" demanded Dale at the same time.

"Let's just say it's organic evidence. Something I saw at your house yesterday when I stopped to get out of the rain. It was the same thing that was found on the floor of Harvey Ruger's room."

"What's this?" Randy asked. "What are you talking about, Mrs. May? What is she talking about, Dale?"

"Shut up, Randy."

"It was a bit of white dandelion fluff; the seed pod with wings that catches on to everything and won't let go. There was a dandelion seed pod caught in the bed ruffle in Mr. Ruger's room."

"So what? Maybe Harvey picked it up somewhere himself. Or Abigail when she went walking in the woods with you that night."

"There wasn't a dandelion on the place anywhere, not even along the path from the Manor House to your cottage, Randy. As a matter of fact, I remarked to Dale yesterday that Ernie did a wonderful job in tending the grounds. The only place I found dandelions was at Dale's place yesterday. Even though they were wet with rain, the little seed pods grabbed my pant leg and clung to it."

"Could have been Ernie; you know, he spends a lot of time at my place."

"But he cuts through the woods in the back of the house; he doesn't come up the driveway where he might be seen. The dandelions were growing by the driveway and in the front yard."

"Dale! Can't you do anything right?" Randy shouted. "I'll tell you the truth, Mrs. May. Dale, if you were in that room, tell us now. Robbing rich people of things they don't even know they have is one thing; murder is another. Did you do it?"

"Of course, I didn't!" Dale shouted back.

Then Randy told Mrs. May the whole story of the theft operation the two of them had been running with Ernie's help ever since the spa had opened.

Harboring resentment at losing the estate, which he considered rightfully his, Dale saw an opportunity when the Clareton Manor became a business that would draw rich clients. The tunnel, unknown to the new buyer, would provide a means to enter the premises undetected. He ran into Ernie Snale, his old childhood playmate, in town one day and encouraged him to apply for work at the spa. After he told Erika he had grown up in the little cottage behind the Manor House, Ernie was hired as a gardener on sentimental grounds. In time, they recruited Randy to join their theft ring. Things were going well; Dale was pleased with his new tax-free business.

Randy sized up the clientele to determine who would be the most likely to have spare cash on him or her. When he got the chance, he went through Erika's mail, looking for information about the financial status of the guests—he thought Chantal had seen him once. Innocent kitchen conversations about who must be "really rich" were picked up by Ernie, either directly or indirectly, through gossip from the hired help. Ernie then passed on the information to Dale.

As a trusted employee, Randy had full access to the Manor House; he used the confidence to have duplicate keys made for all the rooms. During mealtimes, when all the guests were occupied in the dining room, Dale would go to the cottage, get the designated key, sneak through the tunnel, rob the victim—trying to take things that would not be noticed right away, stash the loot and get back to the cottage. Usually he took a ten or twenty dollar bill; rich people never seemed to know exactly how many twenties they had on them anyway, and most of the thefts were never even reported. Occasionally it would be earrings or a cell phone or other small electronics. Sometimes the guests reported a theft, but more often they thought they were having a memory lapse and had not brought the particular item with them or had misplaced it. They averaged only a few hundred dollars worth of loot a week, but it was extra spending money, not taxable, and they both felt they needed and deserved. And there appeared to be no risk. Until Harvey Ruger was murdered.

"What did you steal from Harvey?" Molly asked.

Dale hesitated. "Please tell her, Dale," Randy begged. "Tell her everything!" He was starting to wring his hands in desperation. Dale's being in the Ruger room on the day Harvey was murdered was something he was hearing for the first time; he did not know that Dale had decided to make the snatch earlier than the usual dinner time hour.

With his characteristic haughtiness, Dale reluctantly agreed. "Okay, then. It went like this. By Tuesday morning, Ernie had already let me know that Harvey Ruger was rich. Ernie told me that he was having a massage at three o'clock in the afternoon on Tuesday, so I decided to check out his room then, without waiting 'til dinner time.

"I was headed for my car—I park it beside the road down past the cottage and walk back through the woods when I'm going to the Manor House on business—when I saw the little blue Japanese car go by toward the manor. I waited awhile; I thought it might be a delivery man, flowers or something, and I might run into him. In no time at all, it came back, going real fast.

"It was getting late; I knew I had to hurry, or I wouldn't get in and out before the massage was over. When I got to Ruger's room, the door was ajar. I peeked in through the crack and saw no one, so I pushed it open and saw a man lying on the floor. I couldn't call for help under the circumstances, so I just left. It shook me up, I can tell you. But I didn't know he was dead. I didn't find out until the next day that it was Ruger."

"I think you'd better tell Detective Bloom the whole story as soon as possible," Molly said, getting up off her makeshift stool.

"Yes, let's go, Dale," Randy agreed. "Let's get this over with."

When they emerged from the tunnel into the kitchen of the cottage, they saw Detective Bloom and Officer Windham getting out of an unmarked car outside. Soon the whole story had been retold. Randy and Dale were arrested on the spot, and a uniformed officer was sent to find Ernie.

Molly and Bloom were left standing alone.

33
Dandelion Fluff

"Molly, I just wanted to say thanks for helping us out with Yazid and Stromb. We didn't have grounds to hold them for murder, but we intend to ask them a few more questions—once they get a lawyer. If it's true that Dale saw Harvey on the floor after he saw Tony speed away from the premises, it looks worse for Tony, don't you think?"

"Not at all. Dale didn't tell you the truth when he said he pushed open Harvey's door, saw him on the floor and left. No, indeed. He went into the room. There was a dandelion seed attached to the bed ruffle; I found it Tuesday night when I decided to make sure the search the police made did not miss anything. There are no dandelions growing anywhere on the Manor grounds; the only place around here that I saw dandelions growing was in Dale's front yard by his driveway. He said he drove his car down the lane and parked past Randy's cottage and walked back through the woods. He must have gotten the dandelion fluff on him when he got into his car. In a struggle with Harvey, his leg must have brushed against the bed with enough force to dislodge the seed which then caught in the bed ruffle." She opened her hand to reveal a tiny plastic envelope with a dandelion seed inside.

"Is that so?"

"I don't know if it's enough to convince a jury, but it's enough to convince me. Maybe you can use it to try to get a confession. The motive should be easy enough—Harvey walked in on Dale as the burglary was in progress, a struggle followed, and Harvey ended up dead."

Detective Bloom pulled out his cell phone and dialed a number. "Windham," he said, "get an arrest warrant and a couple of the guys, and go intercept the Right Reverend Dale Stromb before he makes bail on the burglary charge. Hold him on suspicion of murder."

34

Come Saturday Morning

Around mid-morning on Saturday, Detective Bloom and Officer Windham returned to the Clareton Manor Estate. Randy and Ernie had been arrested on charges of burglary, had posted bond and were out. Randy had been allowed to go to Columbia to find a lawyer. No one knew where Ernie was. Dale was being held in the County Jail without bond on suspicion of murder.

Bloom was wearing well-worn jeans and a faded but neatly pressed shirt open at the neck. The few strands of hair over the top of his head were not as neatly plastered as usual. He was waiting for Molly in the parlor.

Upon seeing his garb, she smiled and said, "Casual day at the police department?" She hoped he had a sense of humor.

He did. "I couldn't take that rope wrapped around my neck another day this week," he replied with a laugh.

The arrests of the day before were all the buzz around the Manor House, and the guests were starting to gather in the main hall outside the parlor as Officer Windham left. "Come on in," Molly said, when she saw them.

"Okay, folks," Bloom added. "As you know, we have made an arrest in this case, and I'm sure you're relieved to know that none of you is a suspect any longer. We expect to have a full confession from the Reverend Dale Stromb as soon as his defense attorney approves the deal."

Detective Bloom continued to speak. First he addressed himself to Abigail. "Mrs. Ruger," he said in a resolutely natural voice, "I'm truly sorry for your loss which has been exacerbated by the events of this week. I know you'll be glad to be on your way. You have arrangements to make and a will to have read."

Looking at Tony, who had been released from jail, he added, "We have obtained a copy of the will during the investigation to determine who would benefit from Mr. Ruger's death; it would not be appropriate to go into details, but Mr. Ruger's family is well provided for. Greed is often the motive for murder, and there are good reasons that close family members are prime suspects. The newspapers had you tried and convicted, but you are innocent of this offense. With a search warrant, we were able to have your apartment in New Orleans checked out thoroughly. We found several hundred thousand dollars worth of gold coins. A bank in Spartanburg verified that someone calling himself Harvey Ruger accessed his safe deposit box on Tuesday. What did you come to Clareton Manor for, Tony?"

"The key," Tony said simply. He knew it was over; there was no point in trying to continue the lie. "The key to the safe deposit box. I knew either the gold or the combination to the safe at home had to be in the box.

"Oh, Tony. You know I would have given you money," his mother said with a resigned tone.

"Half a million? Would you have given me half a million? I was tired of living in poverty. I wanted to live a normal, decent life for a change."

Cindy had been holding Tony's hand; now she let it go. Love may cover a multitude of sins, but nobody ever said it covered them all. This was too much. She knew it was over; she could feel it.

The Detective turned to Marcus. "Mr. Bella," he said, "we

owe you an apology. Not only did you suffer insult by the victim himself, we've added injury to that by questioning your integrity without cause. I'm sorry for what you and your wife have been through."

"Apology accepted." The words were hard to get out through teeth that were still tightly clenched, but they were spoken. That was the important thing. Angie reached over to him and gave him a silent hug.

"Mr. and Mrs. Whitt, I'm sorry your vacation has been ruined. And I'm sorry for all you've been through."

Francis just nodded. He and Marian remained seated next to Abigail.

"Ms. Pritchard, we've kept you from your job long enough. I wish there was something we could do to make it up."

"That's okay. You did what you had to do."

Nora cast a brief glance in Molly's direction as she got up to leave; Molly smiled and looked down. She was glad she had not passed on the information she got from Nora about her youthful relationship with Harvey. It had no bearing on the case, and no one needed to know about it.

Erika gave instructions to Peter and Christa to help the guests with whatever they might need to be on their way. "There won't be any lunch today, I'm afraid. Randy is in Columbia."

"That's okay with me," Marcus answered. "I'm going to Subway."

"By the way, Detective," Molly asked. "What ever happened to Barry?"

"Oh, we found him. In Maine. He said he just wanted to get away from it all. Said his life had become one disaster after another, and he had to have some space. We found him in a cheap motel with no one but a book. He has no plans to come back."

Soon the room was empty except for Erika, the Detective, and Molly. Erika said, "Are the autopsy results in? What was the official cause of death?"

"It was ruled as blunt force trauma; that is what they put down as the primary cause. COPD was listed as a secondary cause. His health was not good."

"Chronic Obstructive Pulmonary Disease. Emphysema."

"Yes, years of heavy smoking had interfered with his lungs' ability to supply oxygen to his body and brain. He probably wouldn't have lived more than a couple of years anyway. Or so they said."

"Molly, let's go downtown for lunch. Would you like to join us, Detective?"

"Thanks for the invitation, but I've hardly seen my wife all week. I think she wants me home to cut the grass."

Erika nodded and smiled." Goodbye then. We'll see you later, I'm sure."

35

A Confession or Two

It didn't take long to get a confession from Dale. He had no experience with the police and they soon wore him down.

He admitted that he went into Harvey Ruger's room to rob him, believing that he was in a massage therapy session, as he was told by Ernie. When Harvey came out of the bathroom, he was startled to find a man in his room and began shouting at him angrily, demanding to know what he was doing there. He stepped between Dale and the door, and Dale said he pushed him—harder than he meant to, probably due to the adrenaline rush brought on by the surreptitious entry and subsequent confrontation. Harvey fell backward, tripped, and fell and hit his head on the corner of the open closet door. Dale said he would have made a run for it, but Harvey spun around and grabbed his ankle, and he fell. There was a struggle that ended when inside the closet door, Dale's hand fell upon a dumbbell which found its way to Harvey's head. "I was sure he was still breathing when I left," Dale insisted.

His lawyer advised him that a death that occurs during the commission of a crime is considered murder and would qualify for the death penalty. He could take his chances with a jury or he could make a full confession and accept a plea bargain that would keep him alive. He agreed to plead guilty.

Driving back from town after lunch, Erika and Molly were both silent; Molly noticed that the dogwood trees were already starting to shed the white and pink petals along the lane. Maybe the brevity of spring was essential for its exuberance. In one short week, the pale colors were giving over to the lush green of freshly mowed lawns and trees in full leaf. The azaleas lining the driveway were already starting to show a few blossoms that had been filled with light fading into brown. The cycle of life. Of nature. We all end up the same way, like Harvey. The rich. The poor. All end up the same way.

At last Erika steered the car into the garage and turned off the engine. Without looking up, she said, "Molly, I'm going to the drumming place–I've got to unwind. Will you come with me?"

"Surely," said Molly. Her nerves were stretched tight enough to break; if drumming would help, she'd give it a try.

They walked down the path between the neat rows of trees, the same path they had walked together with Abby and Marian on Tuesday evening, and soon came to the clearing with the rocks and stumps arranged in a circle. The sun was still high in the west; but the thickness of the forest prevented the rays from penetrating the shadows of the circle. Erika lowered herself into a simple cross-legged position and began to pat her hands rhythmically on a tree stump as she closed her eyes and dropped her head. Molly copied her the best she could; she never did have a sense of rhythm. They sat there for a long time.

Finally, Erika spoke. "It's getting a little chilly here in the shade. Ready to head back?"

Molly nodded and arose slowly from her position on the ground. They started back up the path toward the house. Molly could sense that Erika's tension had not been completely eradicated.

"So Harvey had a weak heart and then his head was bashed in. And it happened here, in my place. The spa I worked so long and hard for. Why?"

"It's done. There's nothing left to do but accept it and try to go on from here."

"I'm probably ruined, you know."

"Let go, Erika, just let go. Isn't that what you spent years teaching me to do?"

"There's one more thing."

"What?"

Still continuing in her lethargic pace, Erika sighed and finally spoke. "You were a cop, Molly; you know the law. Is it a crime to disfigure a corpse?" Not waiting for an answer, she continued. "The door was open just a crack and I could see him lying on the floor. My first thought was that he'd pulled something else to ruin the week. Molly, you know how hard and how long I have worked to get this business going. It hasn't been easy. If my guests don't have an enjoyable and relaxing time here, I'll go out of business. After one day here, Harvey Ruger had created so much tension that everyone was miserable. He was ruining everything and there was nothing I could do. I was helpless.

"When Barry told me that he'd cut short his massage, I decided to go to his room and confront him in private. Beg him to understand my position–he was a businessman; I thought he'd understand.

"Then I saw him lying on the floor–in a helpless position himself at last–and I wanted him to suffer. I was glad. Then I came to my senses and called out to him. He didn't answer of course. I went into the room and touched his shoulder; I could tell right away he was dead.

"Then something came over me. I've told you before and I swear it's true that I don't believe in the occult or anything associated with it. But I have done some reading on witchcraft as well as topics related to alternative medicine and all sorts of spiritual matters. And as I looked at Harvey lying dead on the floor, I remembered reading that a wicked soul can be hastened on his way by disfiguring the corpse. I didn't believe it, of course, but I picked up a barbell and I bashed it against his head! Then I just left him there. I know it was wrong of me. But I was full of rage and anger at his hatefulness. And I just did it."

"There's good and bad in everyone," was all that Molly said. Ninety-nine percent of the time it was best not to tell all you know.

About the Author

Kathleen Newberg is a graduate of Southeastern Bible College in Birmingham, Alabama, with a BA degree in foreign missions, and a graduate of North Carolina State University, with a Bachelor of Science degree in electrical engineering. She has worked in human resources with the Federal civil service and as an electrical engineer with a Department of Energy contractor. She became a fan of Agatha Christie in the late 1970's after a co-worker overcame her protests and persuaded her to read one of Christie's books. Since then she has read all of them at least once and has a nearly complete collection of them. This is her first novel.